Lucy Jane at the Ballet

'A wave of laughter rolled up from the
auditorium as the little girl stood motionless at
the side of the stage. On the other side a ballerina
was gracefully dancing, apparently unaware that
a girl was standing in the spotlight looking like a
stunned rabbit and making the audience laugh
. . . "Get off the stage. Quickly!"'

D0588497

The author is sharing her royalties with Tadworth Court Hospital which provides treatment and care for chronically sick and handicapped children

LUCY JANE
AT THE
BALLET

Susan Hampshire
Illustrated by Vanessa Julian-Ottie

Mammoth

First published in 1987
by William Collins Sons & Co Ltd
Magnet paperback edition first published 1988
Reissued 1989 by Mammoth
an imprint of Mandarin Paperbacks
Michelin House, 81 Fulham Road, London SW3 6RB

Mandarin is an imprint of the Octopus Publishing Group

Printed in Great Britain
by Cox & Wyman Ltd, Reading

ISBN 0 7497 0218 4

Contents

The author would like to thank Ann Marriott and Dawn Blackburn for typing the manuscript, Eddie and Elias for listening endlessly to it, and Pat Spooner and Marguerite Porter of the Royal Opera House for all their help and advice.

Lucy Jane at the Ballet was written at Crystal Springs, St James, Barbados

For
Christopher Paris
Celia and Marie
Henrietta, Rose
Daisy, Giannis and Nico
John and Constantine
Alexandra, Virginia and Isabella
and Christina

1

The Theatre Royal

Lucy Jane Tadworth sat beside her father on top of a red London bus on her way to the Theatre Royal, Covent Garden. Her eyes filled with tears. As one rolled down her cheek, she rubbed her woollen gloves across her face and tried to pretend to her father that she was not crying.

Going to live in a theatre for most children would be as exciting as going to live in a castle, but Lucy Jane Tadworth had no desire to be in a theatre as she was sure that theatres were full of ghosts and mice. She wanted to stay at home with her father and look after her kitten, Tilly. But instead, she was to stay with her Aunt Sarah who was the wardrobe mistress at the theatre while her mother went into hospital to have a baby. The doctor had told Mrs Tadworth that she should rest before the baby was born. So Lucy Jane really had no choice. She had to go to stay with her aunt.

"Don't cry, Lucy, it's not for long and you'll

love staying with Sarah," her father said.

Lucy Jane was silent.

"Come on, darling!" Mr Tadworth took his daughter's hand. "The reason Sarah doesn't want to have Tilly to stay as well as you is in case she's naughty. Cats can be very mischievous and Tilly would jump all over the place, perhaps even on the costumes in the theatre wardrobe and . . ." Mr Tadworth tailed off, looking at his daughter.

Lucy Jane thought about her father's words for a moment. Privately she agreed it would be a shame to spoil anything as lovely as a ballet dress – she had seen a picture of one in a book she had been given for Christmas – but she replied rather sadly, "I think Aunt Sarah doesn't want to have Tilly because she doesn't like cats." Then suddenly she threw her arms around her father's neck and pleaded, "Please, Daddy, don't make me go and live in a theatre!"

All the passengers at the top of the bus looked round. Quite unaware of their eyes upon her, Lucy Jane squeezed her father even tighter, saying affectionately, "I'll look after you while Mummy's away. Please – don't make me go."

Mr Tadworth kissed his daughter's brow, slid her comfortingly onto his lap and spoke very softly, so that the people around them could not hear.

"Lucy, darling, theatres are magic places.

You'll see."

He felt sure that his daughter's stay with her Aunt Sarah would be the most exciting holiday of her life, and he tried to console her by adding, "I don't expect you'll want to come home to Mummy and me and the new baby after your lovely stay with Sarah."

Lucy Jane did not answer, she just looked into her lap. Then, as she seemed so sad, her father picked her up and made his way down the stairs of the bus, and they got off at the next stop.

As they walked briskly through Covent Garden on the cold winter morning, Lucy Jane dragged behind her father, holding his hand with both of hers. She grumbled under her breath, "I definitely know Aunt Sarah doesn't like cats."

Her father did not want to argue, so he said nothing and they walked on hurriedly in silence.

As they turned the corner, the great theatre loomed up before them and Mr Tadworth said, "There might be a matinée this afternoon, Lucy. Perhaps your Aunt Sarah can arrange for you to see the show – it's a ballet."

"I don't want to see a ballet. Anyway, my friend Jennie says all that happens in the theatre is pantomines. Children fly around on wires, men dress up as horses, girls pretend to be boys and old men call themselves women," said Lucy Jane and she shuffled her feet along the pavement.

When they arrived at the stage door, Mr Tadworth held a very disgruntled Lucy Jane firmly on one side and her small suitcase on the other.

"Excuse me," he said very politely to the old stage door-keeper. He knew that stage door-keepers could be fierce and he did not want to make a bad impression.

"Can I see my sister, Miss Tadworth, please?"

The old man, eating a biscuit, did not answer. Holding his scruffy mongrel dog on his lap, he looked like a jack-in-the-box as he sat on the high wooden stool in the dark green booth framed by an open window. Pinned all around the walls behind him were dozens of messages, letters, visiting cards and telephone numbers.

"I hope they won't ever need to telephone those

numbers in a hurry," Lucy Jane thought to herself, as she eyed the 999 written in red underneath the words, 'For Police and Fire'. The stage doorkeeper's dog scowled at her suspiciously.

Sarah Tadworth was Lucy Jane's aunt, and as she was in charge of all the costumes for the ballet, she lived in a flat opposite the theatre to be near her work.

Mr Tadworth was a little surprised that the stage door-keeper was not more helpful.

"I would like to see Miss Sarah Tadworth, the wardrobe mistress," he repeated.

"No, sir. Sorry," the old man said gruffly, looking straight at Lucy Jane, "not with that little girl you can't. No children allowed in the theatre after curtain up. Fire regulations."

"Good," Lucy Jane thought. "I won't have to stay." Then she raised her head and pronounced very grandly, "That suits me perfectly. I never wanted to stay in a horrid old theatre in the first place." Her father looked at her severely, he had seldom known her to behave so badly.

"But Miss Tadworth is my sister," he explained, hoping the old man had not heard his daughter's remark. "Please, she's expecting us," he added.

"Well, if she's your sister and she's expecting you, I'll let you in. She did mention that someone was coming with a little girl."

He turned to his mongrel dog and gave him a pat on the head.

"All right then," he mumbled, squinting at Lucy Jane. "Top floor, room marked Wardrobe, but be quick, else I'll have the fireman grumbling about kids in the theatre. Still, I expect our Sarah has got permission for the little one to be here." He was just about to put the biscuit he was holding into his mouth when his dog suddenly snapped it up.

Mr Tadworth thanked the old man and they set off up the five flights of stairs. Lucy Jane followed her father, smiling to herself as she remembered the stage door-keeper's expression when he saw what had happened to his biscuit.

As they trudged up the stairs, Lucy Jane realised that being in a theatre was like being in no other place in the world. Suddenly, three dancers dressed in silver and gold weaved by her with such speed, that Lucy Jane was sure their feet could not have touched the ground. She tried to resist the excitement growing inside her, as she gazed at them open-mouthed. Then four men dressed as harlequins in glittering sequins from head to toe sprang round a corner. They propelled themselves with great ease from one landing to another. Lucy Jane felt a little frightened. Everything was so unexpected, it was almost like being in Aladdin's cave. She wished she could go and peep inside the dressing rooms they passed on each landing, but her father called, "Come on. Keep up, Lucy. Nearly there," so she obediently followed.

By the time she and her father reached the top of the stairs, Lucy Jane no longer thought the theatre a horrid place inhabited by ghosts and mice, but she still had reservations about staying with her Aunt Sarah. Her father knocked at the door marked 'Wardrobe' and Sarah Tadworth, a plump curly-headed woman, opened it. The Wardrobe was not a big wooden cupboard to keep clothes in, as Lucy Jane had expected, but a large room with three washing machines, clothes lines, ironing boards, sewing machines, huge wicker baskets and rail upon rail of ballet dresses and fancy costumes lining the walls.

Aunt Sarah looked very flustered and worried. In one hand she held scissors, in the other a tape measure, she had pins between her lips, and an enormous length of lavender velvet slung over her shoulder.

"Come in, quick, quick!"

With so many pins in her mouth, it was hard to hear what she said. But Mr Tadworth took his daughter's hand and they darted into the room.

"Put Lucy Jane in the skip – the big basket over there, and if anyone comes in, close the lid and pretend she's not here."

Lucy Jane was amazed by her Aunt's strange welcome but she didn't manage to say a word before her aunt continued, "And John, you had better say you've just come for a fitting."

Perhaps she's joking, Lucy Jane thought as her aunt took the pins out of her mouth and walked over to the nearest basket.

"Me, a fitting!" Mr Tadworth laughed. All the time, Lucy Jane kept holding tightly onto her father's hand. Her head was buried in his coat, it smelt lovely. It smelt of Daddy, pipe smoke, after-shave and paint. The thought of her father leaving her at the theatre filled her with fear. She did not want to let go of his hand, but Sarah briskly lifted her into the air, and dropped her into the basket. Then she plonked a ballet dress onto her head.

"Stay there, Lucy Jane, and if someone knocks, keep your head down and I'll close the lid."

Lucy Jane obediently crouched in the skip, the ballet dress still on her head; it looked like an enormous cartwheel hat and was very becoming. Suddenly there was a bang at the door. The tutu slipped down over Lucy Jane's eyes and all you could see was her chin.

"Where's the Rose Queen's dress?" cried a large friendly-looking lady called Lillie as she rushed into the room. "Quick! She's on in a minute."

Lillie was in a terrible panic.

"Angels above," she said. "My lady's there in the altogether except for her tights. Quick!" And she started to look for the dress along the rails.

Mr Tadworth looked over to Lucy Jane. He was pleased that Lillie was in such a fluster that she didn't notice his daughter huddled in the basket. Sarah quickly handed Lillie the Rose Queen's dress and ushered her out of the room. As soon as Lillie had gone, Mr Tadworth opened the lid and said, "Come on Lucy, out you come," and he gave her his hand.

She was about to climb out when Sarah said, "You can leave the lid open, but you'd better stay in there until I have time to take you over to the flat. Lots of people have to come in and out of here during the performance, and children are not supposed to be back-stage without permission. I won't be long." She paused for a moment then added, "I've been so busy, I haven't had time to tell the Company Manager that Lucy Jane is coming to stay, but I will as soon as I have finished cutting out this cloak."

So Lucy Jane stayed where she was. After a minute or two she became very restless and uncomfortably hot, the musty smell of old costumes all around her was making her feel sick. If life in the theatre was going to be like this, she knew she was right not to want to come. When an opportunity came, she would creep out of the basket and run away.

In the meantime, she stayed quietly in position, planning her next move. Her father handed Aunt Sarah the suitcase and tried to reassure her.

"Don't worry, Lucy will be fine as soon as she's found her feet. I'll collect her once Ann is out of hospital, and I can always have her at home on Sunday if you're desperate."

Then he walked over to the skip. "Oh, Lucy darling! You must be roasting in there," and he patted her head and kissed her goodbye. Lucy Jane wanted to beg her father not to go, but instead she just hid under the dresses and tried not to cry. She had resolved to leave the theatre anyway once he had gone, so now it was much better to pretend to be brave. She shut her eyes tightly and thought of home and Saturday sweets.

After Lucy Jane's father had gone, Sarah seemed to forget all about her niece and carried on cutting out the velvet material on the huge table. Lucy Jane could see the back of her aunt's head as she bent over, completely absorbed in her work. This, Lucy Jane knew, was her chance, so she very quietly climbed out of the basket and crept from the room.

As soon as she was outside the Wardrobe, she knew she had to find her way to the stage door. So she scuttled down the five flights of stairs, relieved that not a soul was in sight. "They're probably all on the stage," she thought. But just as she was creeping past the stage door-keeper's booth, the old man's dog began to bark.

Lucy Jane held her breath.

"Who's that?" the old door-keeper said.

"Rats and rabbits!" Lucy Jane said to herself as she was forced to dart back into the theatre. "Just my luck! Barking mongrels stopping me in my tracks – now I don't know where I should go," and she rushed through a huge door marked SILENCE, STAGE, NO SMOKING. She found herself in an enormous dark room, bigger than a church. The sound of an orchestra was drifting through the black space and as she tried to accustom her eyes to the dim surroundings, her heart was banging in her chest. She tiptoed forward not knowing where she was going or what she might discover. Then she noticed long shafts of light some way from where she stood, and she made her way towards them. As she edged nearer, she could see the tall beams of yellow light stretching up to the roof, with long lengths of black material falling between. She peered round the material hoping to discover where the beams of light would lead, and she gingerly stepped forward. Before she realised what had happened, she found herself in a vast brightly lit space, engulfed in a cave of colour and surrounded by lights, trying to see where she was. A wave of laughter rolled up from the auditorium as the little girl stood motionless at the side of the stage. On the other side a ballerina was gracefully dancing, apparently unaware that a girl was standing in the spotlight looking like a stunned rabbit and making the audience laugh. Then suddenly two long, slim legs were dancing very expertly beside Lucy Jane, and the ballerina's voice hissed to her, "Get off the stage. Quickly!"

"What stage?" Lucy Jane said and backed away into the dark, the audience's laughter again ringing in her ears. Filled with embarrassment she covered her head with her hands.

"I've just been on a real stage in front of real people, and I only arrived at the theatre this afternoon," she thought.

Poor Lucy Jane could not believe what had happened to her. Blinded by the footlights, she glanced back at the stage. The lights were so bright she could not see the audience but she could just see the ballerina floating as though nothing had happened, in the rose dress Lillie had collected from the Wardrobe.

"Better not stay here and get caught," Lucy Jane decided and ran as quickly as she could towards a large door underneath a bright green EXIT sign. As she did so, she tripped over some electric cables on the ground and for a second all the lights in the theatre went out. A soft *"Oooh!"* rose from the stalls, and, at the same time, a loud "Rats and rabbits!" came piercing through the dark from Lucy Jane. Then a stern man's voice snapped, "Hush! PLEASE!" Then he cried, "Lights. Put on the emergency lights." The cross voice, ringing round the theatre, sounded extremely fierce and Lucy Jane thought she had better pretend she wasn't there, so she stayed stock still trying to think what she should do next. Suddenly all the lights went back on again and calm was restored.

Despite the lights having gone out and a small child walking onto the stage, the ballerina was still dancing away gracefully in time to the music, her rose dress rippling as she moved. Lucy Jane wanted to stay at the side of the stage and watch, but she knew she had to get away from the stern voice, so she crept on towards the big EXIT door and heaved it open. On the other side she found herself in a long corridor. It had a dark red carpet, red walls, and doors all along one side. She walked up to the first door, which had a small gold crown painted on it. Men in dark suits were standing outside. They were so tall, they did not notice Lucy Jane slip between them and quietly push open the door. She put her head inside and without thinking, darted into the room, closing the door after her. When she turned round, she

was surprised to find there were two ladies sitting
watching the ballet from the balcony of the tiny
room which overlooked the stage.

"Oh, who are you?" said a beautiful young
woman sitting on the gilt chair nearest the stage.
She was wearing a blue silk dress and had three
strands of pearls tight around her throat. She
could have been a princess, she was so pretty.

The young woman held out her hand to Lucy
Jane and whispered, "What are you doing here?"

Lucy Jane couldn't answer.

"Are you lost?"

Lucy Jane still didn't speak.

"Gracious me!" the beautiful girl exclaimed softly. "I know! – You're the tiny person I've just seen on stage. But why are you here?"

Lucy Jane gazed up and said nothing. She felt very lost and small as she took the hand stretched out towards her, and shyly edged her way nearer to the lady in the silk dress. When she peered over the balcony, she could see the whole stage bathed in light and the ballerina being carried majestically on the shoulders of a tall man in a bright red velvet jacket.

What a beautiful sight! She could hardly believe her eyes. She gazed at the stage in wonder. Suddenly, the lights in the auditorium came up and everyone was clapping and a man wearing a dark green uniform with gold braid and brass buttons came into the little room, bowed and murmured, "Tea will be served in the anteroom." He bowed again and flattened himself against the wall to make way for the ladies to pass.

The beautiful young woman in the silk dress rose from her chair, tucked her handbag under her arm, and whispered to the tall lady accompanying her, "Annabelle, will you see that this little one is taken care of," and she looked down and smiled at Lucy Jane.

"It's all right, I live here," Lucy Jane said half-truthfully, and she curtsied and darted from the room before anyone could stop her. She ran along the plush red carpeted corridor, down the stairs, through the large foyer and out on to the front step of the theatre. There she sat with her chin cupped in her hands.

"Now," she thought, as she arranged herself comfortably on the cold step. "Do I really want to run away from this theatre? It's not been a bad day, except that I'm hungry. I've just seen a ballet, appeared on a stage, held the hand of a lady who looked like a princess, and seen a Wardrobe full of more fancy dresses than anyone in my school could imagine. And this is only my first day!" With that thought, she drew herself up, stepped back and looked at the huge theatre destined to be her temporary home.

"Yes," she thought, "I'm going to stay. I'm going to find my Aunt Sarah and I'm going to enjoy this holiday," and she walked back out of the cold and into the theatre.

2
Meeting a ballerina

Lucy Jane found her way from the front of the theatre along the same red corridor, and back through a large door called the pass-door which led from the auditorium to back-stage. When she was at the side of the stage once again, trying to find her way to her Aunt Sarah, she bumped into a dancer. The dancer, wearing huge woolly leg warmers and a pink shawl wrapped around her shoulders, looked at Lucy Jane.

"Good heavens!" she exclaimed in a soft deep voice. "It's you!"

Lucy Jane looked up and smiled. "Yes, it is me. I'm lost," she said.

It did not occur to the little girl that the ballerina might be cross with her, and she repeated rather cheekily, "Yes, I am very lost as a matter of fact!"

The ballerina shook her head, too annoyed to speak, then she said sternly, "You must never,

never walk onto a stage when there's a performance on, even if you ARE lost." Now the ballerina
was so cross her voice sounded quite foreign.

Lucy Jane felt rather confused.

"What stage?" she asked, "Oh yes, this stage.
But you see, I didn't know it was a stage until I
was on it. I've never been behind the scenes in a
theatre before."

Although the ballerina had been very angry and
was quite exhausted by the huge row that had
broken out in the interval on account of the little
girl, she nevertheless decided that it was best to
try to protect Lucy Jane from coming face to face

with the furious Company Manager. So she
hurried the small culprit away from the scene of
the crime. She took Lucy Jane's hand and,
avoiding the scenery, the ballerina led her quickly
across the dark back-stage.

The short cut to the ballerina's dressing room
passed the scenery dock where all the sets for the
ballets were stored, and then through the prop
room, where extra thrones and carriages, crowns,
and carts filled with flowers were kept for the
different ballets. As soon as Lucy Jane entered the
prop room, she let out a terrified scream. A huge
black bear was standing, large as life, in the
corner.

"A bear!" stammered Lucy Jane. The dancer
laughed and lifted Lucy Jane up so she could touch
the stuffed creature standing with his claws bared.

"It's not real – everything in this room is
pretend, all made to look real. Look at this. When
you are sitting in the theatre it looks like a genuine
treasure chest filled with genuine jewels, but it's
only coloured stones and gold paint."

Lucy Jane was a little disappointed that nothing
was really REAL but before she could look
around any more, the ballerina took her through a
small door and led her quickly into her dressing
room. The room was extremely colourful, filled
with flowers, bright lights, costumes and greetings cards.

"Well, well, the trouble you've caused!" the dancer said once they were inside. Although the ballerina came from Russia and was called Tatiana Marova, she sounded almost English except when she was cross. She just spoke a little more softly and deeply and pronounced her words more carefully than most of the people Lucy Jane knew. She took off her shawl, then she sat Lucy Jane on a big, soft and rather old armchair next to her Persian cat, Miss Softpaws. They both looked at Lucy Jane for a long time, then the ballerina said, "My goodness! You're the naughty one. You can not imagine what I would do to you if you were my child."

Lucy Jane felt rather afraid.

"I have no children of my own, but if I had, and they walk on the stage while I am dancing . . . My! I would be cross! And do you know we had a very important person in the Royal Box this afternoon?"

"Yes, I know," Lucy Jane chirped in earnestly, "She held my hand and talked to me."

The ballerina stared at Lucy Jane in surprise. At that moment, there was a knock on the door and before the ballerina had time to say "Come in," Lucy Jane had jumped from her chair and hidden in the cupboard.

"Child! What are you doing?" the dancer asked in amazement.

"I'm hiding in case there is a fire but if it's my Aunt Sarah, don't tell her I'm here because I want to creep back up to the Wardrobe when she's not looking."

At last the ballerina understood.

"Of course," she said. "You are Sarah's little niece, who's coming to stay. Your mother is having a baby."

"Yes, but please don't tell my aunt I'm here," Lucy Jane whispered and squashed herself further into the clothes in the cupboard.

"I don't know what I'll tell her yet," the ballerina said, "But you had better know that it's only *during* a performance children aren't allowed back-stage, in case there is a fire. The reason is that the theatre fireman has to know how many people are in the theatre, so if there *is* a fire, a small child is not left behind as everyone rushes to get out. Fire regulations – that's why you have to get special permission to stay."

Lucy Jane was not really listening, she was so worried about her aunt that she stayed huddled in the cupboard. Nothing could be seen of her except the tip of her hair ribbon and a shoe. There was another knock at the door. Lucy Jane held her breath.

"Miss Marova?" called a familiar voice. "Are you there? Do you want your fitting?"

"Yes, come in," the ballerina said.

From inside the cupboard, Lucy Jane could see her aunt holding up a beautiful dress. All the colours of the rainbow flowed in soft stripes, with chiffon panels falling like a waterfall from the waist. Lucy Jane wished with all her heart she could see the dress a little better, but her aunt kept standing in the way. From the little she could see of the dress, she thought it looked like a beautiful shimmering butterfly costume.

Tatiana Marova was debating in her mind if she should tell Sarah now that her niece was here, or if she should wait. She wanted to befriend Lucy Jane but on the other hand she did not want to see Sarah upset.

Lucy Jane was obviously much on Sarah's mind, for the first words she said as she helped the ballerina to try on the new dress were, "Have you seen a little girl running around anywhere?"

The ballerina could not think how best to answer. But as it happened, Sarah didn't wait for Tatiana to reply and carried on, "My niece, Lucy Jane, is staying with me and the last time I saw her she was upstairs in the Wardrobe. Heaven knows where she is now. She can't be far, but I've looked everywhere."

Miss Marova tried to hide a small smile. She realised that Sarah had no idea that Lucy Jane had actually been on stage during the performance and tripped over one of the main wires, unplugging

31

all the lights, so that for a moment the stage had been in total darkness.

Sarah continued studying the new dress.

"I've so much to do," she said, "all the dresses to finish for the Royal Gala in two weeks. Now they say the Queen *and* all the Royal Family are coming back-stage afterwards. I must say, the child's mother has chosen a fine time to have a baby!" and she frowned and carried on pinning up the hem of Miss Marova's dress.

Lucy Jane, who had heard every word, felt very sheepish. As she edged further into the cupboard, her nose tucked into the dresses and made her want to sneeze. She pinched her nostrils hard with her fingers and made a little choking sound.

Sarah looked up from her work.

"Have you brought Miss Softpaws in today?"

"Yes," the dancer answered very quickly, knowing it was not really her cat who had sneezed. She added casually, "She is probably sleeping under the chair – she usually does on matinée days."

Luckily the ballerina did not need to say another word because Lillie, the stout dresser, burst into the room balancing a tray of tea.

"Your tea, Miss Marova, and your new satin shoes for tonight. I'll draw the curtains, turn up the heater and when Sarah's finished, you can rest."

She fussed around tidying up the dressing table. The last thing the ballerina wanted was for Sarah or Lillie to stay in the room. She feared that at any minute her little friend in the cupboard might be discovered.

"Leave the dress now – it looks perfect," said the ballerina, encouraging Sarah to go. "Let's hope you find that your niece has been waiting up in the Wardrobe all the time," she added with a twinkle in her eye as she managed to usher the two ladies out of the room. At last she was alone. Now to decide the best way to deal with Lucy Jane.

"You see, you naughty one, your aunt is worried out of her mind," she said as she went over and opened the cupboard door, "I intend to put her out of her misery."

"Will I get into trouble?" Lucy Jane asked, thinking that perhaps her aunt might ring her father and send her home. The ballerina said she did not know.

"That is up to your aunt," she said and she picked up the receiver and asked for the Wardrobe.

"Can I speak to Sarah, please?"

There was a long pause and eventually the ballerina said, "All right then, I'll call her when she's finished," and she put down the telephone.

"You're lucky – she's busy so we'll have to ring her later."

"What are you going to do with me?" Lucy Jane asked in a worried voice. She looked quite worn out and Miss Marova suddenly felt sorry for her.

"Well, I'm going to try and get you out of trouble, if you make me a big promise to be good."

"I want to be," Lucy Jane said, shuffling her feet. "If I am good, will I be allowed to watch you dancing tonight?"

"Heavens above!" the ballerina exclaimed, "Bargains from babies!" and she shook her finger at the little girl.

"I'm not a baby," Lucy Jane protested, "I'm eight as a matter of fact – everyone says I'm very grown up for my age."

She flopped back into the large well-worn armchair exhausted from her short speech and, without any warning, lay back her head and fell fast asleep. Then Miss Softpaws, the ballerina's cat, jumped up on the little girl's lap and she too snuggled down and fell asleep. The ballerina looked at them amazed. This was a perfect moment for Miss Marova to find Sarah and put her mind at rest, so she picked up the receiver and tried once again to get through to the Wardrobe. This time, Sarah answered, and Miss Marova spoke to her very quietly so as not to wake the little girl.

"It's all right, Sarah, I've got her here. She's fast asleep. Don't worry, dear, she just got lost. Yes, yes, I'll ring you later when she's awake." She silently replaced the receiver, leaving Sarah greatly reassured.

Lucy Jane was in a deep sleep and dreaming she was the youngest dancer on the stage. Wearing a blue knee-length ballet dress drawn up at one side by a rosette of flowers and a strap of forget-me-nots over the shoulder, she pirouetted on point, while fifty cats just like Miss Softpaws in fifty different costumes danced around her. As our heroine turned, the ribbons from her hair streamed down her back and floated in the air. Her brilliant solo with thirty-two fouetté turns on point ended with cheers from the audience and cries of "Bravo, Lucy Jane! Bravo!" At that moment, Miss Softpaws stirred and Lucy Jane woke with a start. At first she did not know where she was, then she heard the cat purring and her tummy rumbling, and she knew that she was not only hungry, but sitting in a strange room with a strange cat. She slipped off the chair, made her way towards the door and bumped straight into the dressing table.

"Oh rabbits! What's that? Where am I?"

The ballerina, who was relaxing on her couch, opened her eyes.

"What's the matter, Lucy Jane? Can't you see?

It's not very dark – it's just that you're not used to the room. You're here, with me."

"Where's here?" Lucy Jane said, "And who's me?"

The dancer laughed.

"Of course, I know you're not my Mummy," the little girl said quickly, "but I can't remember where I am. I'm not frightened, it's just . . ." and her tummy rumbled again, this time very loudly. Lucy Jane tried to stop it.

Miss Marova turned on the dressing table light and smiled, a warm pleasing smile, and everything flooded back into Lucy Jane's mind.

"So who's got a rumbling tummy?" the dancer said, "Well, we'll have to do something about that," and she called Lillie into the room.

"Lillie, please can you get our little friend here something to eat and bring me my usual toasted steak sandwich. And Lillie," the dancer added, "if you see Sarah, please can you tell her that her niece is now awake."

"Oh!" Lillie exclaimed, looking at Lucy Jane. "The little daredevil! Hide and seek everywhere it's been. I know all about you," and she chuckled away, her chest heaving up and down inside her jumper as she did so. "Now what's your name, lovey?"

"Lucy Jane. Excuse me, please tell me, what is the ballerina's name?"

"Miss Marova's name is Miss Marova," the dresser stated very correctly.

"Tatiana Marova," the dancer interrupted, "but please call me Tati, most people do." And so saying, she rose to her feet and spun round, her arms gracefully above her head. Lucy Jane eyed her with wonder.

"Ooooh! I'd love to dance like that! I'd love to, Miss Marova, I mean Tati. Do you think I could?"

Tatiana Marova, the great ballerina, thought for a moment, then said, "We'll have to see what your aunt says – if she agrees, I could give you a short lesson tomorrow, before I have my own class."

"Hurray, I'm going to learn to dance proper ballet. Hurray! Hurray!" Lucy Jane shouted, as Lillie hurried out of the room for the food, and to tell Sarah that her niece was safe and enjoying life in Dressing Room Number One.

When Lillie came back with the food, Lucy Jane was dancing about the room pretending to be Miss Marova, and Miss Marova was leaning back in the old armchair, laughing and laughing. It really pleased Lillie to see the ballerina so carefree. She often felt that although Tatiana was very successful, her life was lonely and rather hard – all practice, rehearsal, performances and being in the theatre every day and night. She never had a chance to take a proper holiday or "get out of herself" as Lillie called it. So Lillie thought Lucy Jane's visit would not only bring some everyday happiness into Tatiana's world, but also some sparkle to the Theatre Royal.

3
Watching from the wings

Early that evening the whole theatre buzzed with activity. Ballet dancers were hurrying along the corridors, gentlemen of the orchestra just back from high tea were tuning up under the stage and the dressers, their arms laden with costumes, panted up and down the stairs. And in the star's dressing room, Lucy Jane waited patiently, her heart pounding with excitement, longing to know if she was going to be allowed to watch the ballet of 'Cinderella' that evening. As Lillie rushed about the room with head-dresses and tights, hair pins and ballet shoes, Lucy Jane felt sure she hadn't even noticed her sitting there. Miss Marova had gone out into the corridor to talk to Sarah and it seemed to Lucy Jane that everyone was so busy, they had forgotten all about her. At last Miss Marova and Sarah returned. They stood by the door, and stared at Lucy Jane sitting in the old armchair and looking quite angelic. She held Miss Softpaws on her lap and peered up at them hopefully. But the ladies were silent. Lucy Jane waited. After a very long pause, Lucy Jane could contain herself no longer.

"What are you going to do to me, Aunt Sarah? Are you very cross? Am I going to be allowed to watch the ballet?"

Her aunt did not answer her straight away, instead she ran her fingers through her unruly hair. She had been extremely worried and Lucy Jane had been very naughty, but she did not want to scold her niece in front of other people. Before she had time to answer, Lucy Jane asked again, "Aunt Sarah, am I allowed to watch the ballet tonight?"

"Well, Lucy Jane, we have decided . . ." her aunt said, and she gave Tatiana a quick look, then continued, "We have decided to ask the Company Manager what he thinks."

"Yes, we're going to let him decide," the ballerina agreed.

Lucy Jane hung onto the cat and bit her lip.

"What is a Company Manager?" she asked herself. "What does he do? Does he dance? Is he something to do with POLICE? Whoever he is, please everyone in Heaven, let him say I can stay in the theatre and see Tatiana dance tonight."

There was a bang at the door and before anyone could say, "Come in," a tall thin man in a dinner jacket strode into the room. He was the Company

Manager and responsible for everyone back-stage.

"Now," he said, looking over everyone's head and straightening his black bow tie, "I hear some child wants to watch 'Cinderella' from the wings?"

"Yes, I do," interrupted Lucy Jane.

The Company Manager ignored her completely and carried on as though no one had spoken. "I'm not at all keen on having children at the side of the stage unless it's absolutely necessary. However, as you, Miss Marova, have asked me as a special favour, and Sarah, as she is your niece, I find it difficult to refuse. But let us not forget what happened last time this young lady was back-stage!" and he looked straight at Lucy Jane, pausing for a moment. "I'd be grateful," he continued, "if the child in question did not eat sweets, talk, fidget, or move from her position without my permission. And if she can abide by these rules, make sure she reports to me half an hour before the show."

He looked at the two ladies and left the room. When the door was closed, Lucy Jane threw herself into her aunt's arms and kissed her and then she hugged and kissed the ballerina.

"Thank you, thank you both. I'm so happy I'm going to see the ballet. I'm sorry about making you worried out of your mind, Aunt Sarah, but now I'll be as good as a mouse and quiet as an angel."

"Is that a promise?" her aunt enquired and gave her a little shake as though to warn her. "You'd better behave yourself this time my girl, or else . . . big trouble!"

That evening, watching the ballet 'Cinderella' was the most wonderful experience of Lucy Jane's life.

She sat on a high stool next to the stage manager as he organised the show. By pressing buttons and switching on lights on a large board, he made sure the dancers were on time, that the lights were right and that the scenery and curtains operated as they should. Now and then he spoke into a little microphone which could be heard through the loudspeakers in the dressing rooms or in the electricians' lighting box.

Lucy Jane did not move a muscle the whole performance. The dancing, the clothes and the music were all so beautiful, she was carried away into another world. When the dancers came into the wings, they always had a smile or pat on the cheek for their little pig-tailed friend.

In the interval, Geoffrey, the dancer who was playing Prince Charming, came to Lucy Jane's side, kissed her twice and waltzed away. Her cheeks turned very red, but she did not dare say a word or touch her face, as she knew the Company

Manager had forbidden her to move.

Even Tatiana Marova, who was Cinderella, had time for Lucy Jane. She floated from the stage as though she had wings and gave Lucy Jane a smile and a hug. But poor Lucy Jane hardly dared breathe in case the Company Manager forbade her to watch the second half of the performance.

At the end of the ballet she completely forgot all the do's and don'ts and started to clap and cheer enthusiastically. She was just about to jump down from her stool and rush across the stage to the ballerina, when Sarah, who was by now standing behind her, whispered, "Don't move, Lucy Jane! Stay where you are," and she was very glad she did, because when all the cheering had stopped, the ballerina left the stage carrying three huge bouquets of flowers, and came straight over to Lucy Jane and kissed her.

"I'll see you tomorrow to give you your first ballet lesson. Be at the stage door at ten o'clock, don't be late, and if Sarah can find some practice clothes for you, all the better," she said.

And before Lucy Jane had time to thank her, Tatiana gave her a broad smile, the dresser wrapped a pink crochet shawl round her shoulders, and the star was gone.

Although it was very late, Lucy Jane was still extremely excited and didn't feel tired. When her aunt told her that they must go across the road to her flat, Lucy Jane pleaded, "I don't feel at all sleepy, Aunt Sarah – can't we go out and see Covent Garden at night?"

Sarah had been working very hard all day and evening and was quite tired herself so she had no intention of letting her niece stay up any later, especially as Miss Marova was giving her a ballet lesson the following morning. They also had the problem of finding Lucy Jane some ballet clothes by ten o'clock so she hurried her niece across the road.

Aunt Sarah's flat on the fourth floor was very small and brightly decorated, with plants in pots on every surface. There was only one bedroom so Lucy Jane had to sleep on the sofa in the sitting room. But the sofa was very big and squashy and it was already made up into a bed with yellow sheets, and a pillow case with daisies all around the edge.

"Would you like some hot milk to drink before you go to sleep? Or a biscuit?" Sarah asked.

Lucy Jane was still full of the events of the day so she decided to say "yes" to her aunt so that she could stay up a little longer and talk about the ballerina and watching 'Cinderella'.

When Lucy Jane had changed into her nightie with the picture of a clown on the front, she sat down next to Sarah on the edge of the sofa, and drank her warm milk with honey. As she ate her digestive biscuit her feet stroked the furry rug covering the floor. Then she practised pointing her toes, to show her aunt that she had already taken ballet lessons and was going to do her best for Tatiana Marova the next day.

"Why do you think Miss Marova hasn't any children?" Lucy Jane asked suddenly.

"I don't know," Sarah replied. "I think she's too busy and anyway she's not married."

"Oh," Lucy said quietly. "Then I wonder why she's not too busy to like me?"

"Probably *because* she hasn't got any children," Sarah answered. "If she did have any, I expect she'd like a little girl just like you, only not so naughty."

Lucy Jane laughed and with that happy thought snuggled down into her soft sofa bed. Sarah was just about to kiss her goodnight when Lucy Jane said, "I've forgotten to do my teeth!"

So she jumped up and rushed to the bathroom, happy to have an excuse to stay up a little longer.

"Where does Miss Marova live and why does she talk in a special way?" Lucy Jane asked, her mouth full of toothbrush and toothpaste. "Does Miss Softpaws go home with her or does she live in the theatre?"

"Too many questions too late at night," her aunt said. "I'll answer them all in the morning," and with that Lucy Jane was hustled back into the sitting room. As she got into bed, she said suddenly, "I've forgotten my tickly-rug. It's in my suitcase."

Lucy Jane's tickly-rug was the corner of an old blanket she'd had when she was a baby and it had become something of a mascot and went everywhere with her. She loved to hold it close when she went to sleep.

"It's got a lovely smell," Lucy Jane confided to

Sarah as she took it out of the case. "Mummy put some of her scent on it before she left and Daddy said I could put some of his after-shave on too. So it smells like Mummy and Daddy."

And with that, Lucy Jane snuggled into her squashy bed with her tickly-rug, and fell fast asleep.

4

The outing

The next morning Lucy Jane woke to the sound of traffic in the street below. Taxis hooting, police cars' sirens wailing and the noise of people talking and shouting. She jumped out of bed and crept over to the window. She looked down onto the busy street, and watched the passing milk carts and men pushing barrows of fruit. The winter sun was hidden on the other side of the Theatre Royal and the large theatre loomed before her and looked very impressive indeed.

Sarah's voice called out from the kitchen, "Are you awake, Lucy? Do you want to come into the kitchen for breakfast?"

Lucy Jane stayed a moment longer looking out of the window.

"Lovely London," she said to herself, then "Coming, Aunt Sarah, just coming," she shouted as she rushed to join her aunt.

Both Sarah and Lucy Jane ate breakfast very

quickly. A soft boiled egg, toast and honey, and two glasses of orange juice each. Then Lucy Jane dressed so that she could go with Sarah to get the ballet clothes. Although she had gone to sleep rather late, she didn't feel at all tired. Just excited.

The prospect of going to buy some ballet shoes and then going up to the Wardrobe to see if there were any practice clothes that she could use until Sarah had time to make some, or her father could send her own, filled Lucy Jane with delight.

By ten o'clock, Lucy Jane was waiting at the stage door as arranged. Tatiana had planned to give her a ballet lesson in the rehearsal room under the stage, while Sarah was busy with her usual wardrobe mistress duties, washing the tights, at least forty pairs, repairing the costumes and pressing the dresses for the evening's performance.

At half past ten, the great lady had still not appeared. The stage door-keeper took pity on Lucy Jane and very kindly let her wait in his booth because it was so cold by the door. She stood holding her new ballet clothes and absent-mindedly stroking his dog, wondering if she was waiting on the right day.

By a quarter to eleven, at least fifteen dancers from the *corps de ballet* had hurried in from the street and gone downstairs for the ballet class at eleven o'clock.

"It's possible," the old man said, "that Miss Marova could have passed by and not noticed you." It was true that all that was visible of Lucy Jane from outside the cubbyhole was the top of her head.

"But on the other hand," he went on, "if Miss Marova has come in, I certainly would have seen her. So, in my opinion, she's still on her way. I'll keep a good lookout for her."

As time went by, the old man and the little girl had become so friendly that the door-keeper asked Lucy Jane to call him by his first name, Dave. And when an hour later, there was still no sign of Miss Marova's car, Dave begged Lucy Jane to go back upstairs to her aunt in the Wardrobe. He felt sure that the dancer was not going to appear.

"But, Dave, she promised me she'd come," Lucy Jane insisted.

"Yes, but it's after eleven o'clock, my girl, soon be my lunch time," and he rustled his sandwiches wrapped in grease-proof paper under the little girl's nose.

"I've got my dancing shoes, she can't have forgotten me," Lucy Jane said, fighting back the tears. She had hardly slept all night for thinking about getting the practice clothes and having a ballet lesson with Miss Marova the next morning. "I'm staying here," she said determinedly, "that is, if you'll let me, Dave?" and she looked at him pleadingly.

The stage door-keeper looked down at Lucy Jane and chucked her under the chin. He felt quite sorry for her.

"Cheer up! She's forgotten you and that's all there is to it," he said kindly, but for Lucy Jane those were the cruellest words she could hear.

"She's *not* forgotten me," she insisted. The lump in her throat was now so big it hurt, and she could hardly swallow.

"Tell you what," the old man said comfortingly, "Your dad gave me a quid as he left – I'll share it with you. We can buy some sweets."

Lucy Jane knew this was extremely generous but she did not want to buy anything; all she wanted was to see Miss Marova walk safely through the stage door. So she just said, rather dully, "No, thank you."

"Well, if she's not forgotten you, she's nearly forgotten," the old man said.

"I know she has not forgotten me," Lucy Jane replied emphatically, "You don't forget a friend – I AM HER FRIEND," and she hid her face in her ballet clothes and started to cry.

Yet another hour passed, and Lucy Jane was still standing at the stage door, growing graver and more determined by the minute. She was blue with cold. The old man had done his best to persuade her not to wait any longer, but Lucy Jane's mind was made up.

Eventually, the telephone rang. Lucy Jane's heart leapt, was this Miss Marova? Then she heard her aunt's voice asking the stage door-keeper if the Blue Bird dress had come back from the cleaners and her hopes fell.

"No, nothing's arrived this morning," Dave said. "Not even Miss Marova," he added and waited for the penny to drop.

"What?" came the horrified cry at the other end of the line. "Is Lucy Jane still waiting?"

"Yes, she's still waiting, and has been for nearly three hours. She's determined not to move."

"I'll come down," Sarah said and in no time she was at the stage door, her sleeves rolled up and a tape measure still hanging round her neck.

"What on earth can have happened to Tatiana? I do hope she's all right, Dave," she said to the stage door-keeper, "You'd better ring her home and if she isn't there, then contact the Company Manager. I'll take Lucy Jane round the corner for something to eat," and she ran back upstairs to get her purse.

When she returned, Lucy Jane was even more adamant that she would wait for Tatiana and she positioned herself on the stage door step, and sat there huddled up in the cold.

"I'm staying here until Miss Marova comes and that's that," Lucy Jane stated resolutely, and she plonked her new shoes and leotard on the step beside her.

"Oh dear," Sarah said, wrestling in her mind as to whether she should be firmer with her niece.

"Oh, Lucy Jane, you're hopeless!" she said finally and ran round the corner to get 'Miss-Not-Going-To-Move' something to eat.

"What's the time, Dave?" asked a little voice choked up with tears.

"One o'clock," he replied.

"Haven't you got through to Miss Marova yet?"

"Still trying."

Some minutes later he appeared on the step next to Lucy Jane. His dog followed.

"Well," he said gravely. "It's bad news. She left well over three hours ago and her secretary said she was on her way to meet a small child at the theatre. Must be you? And that's all the news I have." He looked very gloomy.

Lucy Jane thought that the news was rather good, at least the ballerina had not forgotten her, and she jumped up saying, "You see, I knew she wouldn't forget me." Then she asked anxiously, "But where is she? Is she hurt?" She was seized by an overwhelming fear that something dreadful had happened to the ballerina.

When Sarah reappeared, she had a hamburger and a milk shake wrapped in a small paper carrier bag and gave it to Lucy Jane.

"What would your mother say if she could see you sitting on the stage door step in the freezing cold eating this rubbish. Now come up to the Wardrobe, Lucy Jane."

She put out her hand. Lucy Jane reluctantly stood up, but she didn't want to leave the stage door. She knew that if she stayed there she would be the first person to see the great dancer when she arrived. And she also knew that she would be the first person the great dancer would see.

The stage door telephone rang again. The old man answered it and then rushed excitedly round to the little girl.

"It's for you, duckie. I think it's HER!" he said meaningfully.

Lucy Jane flew to the telephone, picked up the receiver and waited, holding her breath.

"Yes? Yes? Hallo, it's me."

She was so nervous she wasn't sure what to say.

"Hallo," said a faint voice. "Lucy Jane, it's Tati."

"Oh, Miss Marova, where are you? Are you all right? I'm waiting at the stage door for you."

The voice still sounded very faint and Lucy Jane could only just hear.

"Oh, Lucy Jane, I'm so sorry, but there's been an accident, a taxi bumped into my car, and although I'm not hurt, I had rather a shock, so they made me go to the hospital."

Lucy Jane couldn't even speak, she was so upset.

"Are you still there?" Tati said.

"Yes," she answered in a very quiet worried voice.

"Don't you worry, I'm all right now, they gave me tea, and I shall hire a car and come to the theatre."

"Oh no, don't do that! Don't drive a car." Lucy Jane pleaded.

She heard Tati laugh.

"The car has a driver. I'll be driven to the

theatre. I will see you soon."

When the ballerina arrived, everyone was waiting at the stage door to welcome her: the Company Manager, the ballet mistress, Sarah, Lillie, four of the dancers from the *corps de ballet*, the stage door-keeper, his dog, Geoffrey who played Prince Charming, and of course Lucy Jane. They gave a spontaneous round of applause as she stepped from the car, then they all rushed to greet her. She looked rather pale and Lucy Jane wanted to help her, but the Company Manager pushed everyone aside and led Tatiana to her dressing room. Lucy Jane followed, still holding her new ballet clothes, and the stage door-keeper's dog hurried along after them, greatly enjoying all the excitement. The Company Manager opened the dressing room door for the great ballerina and Lucy Jane, but left the poor dog standing outside in the corridor.

"We have asked the doctor to come and see whether you are well enough to dance tonight," said the very worried Company Manager, as he helped Miss Marova onto her couch. He glanced at Lucy Jane as much as to say, she had no right to be there.

"Now lie still, Miss Marova," he continued, "And I'll tell Lillie to come to you. It's probably best if you don't have anyone here." He paused. "No distractions," he added, throwing Lucy Jane

yet another meaningful glare, and swept out of the room.

While Miss Marova waited for the doctor, the little girl showed Tati her new ballet shoes, leotard and tights.

"These are my practice clothes. I thought they were the most beautiful things in the world, but now you're not well, nothing seems lovely any more."

The dancer smiled and touched the little girl's cheek.

"Why don't you run upstairs to Sarah and put your lovely new clothes away. I'll ring you in the Wardrobe when the doctor has seen me." And she lay her head back, looking very pale. Lucy Jane did as she was told.

Patiently sitting in the Wardrobe for one more hour waiting for Miss Marova to call seemed to Lucy Jane like waiting for five days. She positioned herself next to the telephone, praying for it to ring.

"What do you think the doctor will say?" Lucy Jane asked her aunt as she placed her hand tentatively on the telephone. "What will the doctor do to her? Do you think Tati will be able to dance tonight?"

Lucy Jane was so worried about her friend she did not hear her aunt murmur, "I'm not sure," and she continued: "Will she ever be well enough to give me a ballet lesson?"

Her heart beat faster and faster as she waited for Sarah, who was ironing a ballet dress, to stop what she was doing and reply to her question.

"Lucy, darling, I told you I'm not sure," her aunt repeated. "I expect the doctor will know exactly what Tati should do for the best. But I'm sure she's not badly hurt. Just a little shocked or shaken as they say. You know how it is when you've had a fright. Don't worry. She'll be all right." Sarah put down the iron and went over to her niece.

"Would you like a sweet?" she asked kindly. "I know they're not good for your teeth, but I've got a jar of barley sugars and chocolate mints hidden in the skip for times when I need a treat. Would you like some?"

"I do feel a sweet would be lovely now that I'm feeling a bit shocked and shaken," Lucy Jane replied, repeating Sarah's words, which made Sarah laugh.

"Well, come over here, Miss Shocked and Shaken, and help yourself to some sweets from my secret jar."

Just as Lucy Jane slipped her small hand into the jar to pick out a sweet, the telephone rang. She dropped the jar of sweets into the skip and ran to answer the telephone.

"I'll get it, I'll get it. I expect it's Tati for me,

Aunt Sarah," and sure enough it was.

Tati's quiet deep voice at the other end of the line reassured the little girl.

"I've got a wonderful plan, Lucy Jane."

Lucy Jane held her breath.

"The doctor told me I should have a quiet evening at home to rest and then work again tomorrow. But I feel that I would like to go out to tea first. Do you know what we'll do?"

Lucy Jane didn't dare answer.

"To make up for your disappointment this morning," Miss Marova continued, "I'm going to take you to the Savoy Hotel for tea."

Lucy Jane had never heard of the Savoy Hotel, but it sounded terribly exciting and the fact that it was Miss Marova who was going to take her made it the best surprise she could ever have had.

"That will be lovely, Tati. I'd love to have tea at the Hotel Savoy. Thank you." She put down the receiver, ran over to her aunt and cried, "Tati's taking me out to tea."

"How lovely. Quickly let me do your hair," Sarah said.

"No time for that," Lucy Jane replied, beaming from ear to ear. "She's waiting." She hugged her aunt, grabbed her coat, and dashed down the stairs.

Tatiana Marova was standing by her dressing room door wrapped in her long fur cape and everyone was crowded around her.

"Goodbye, Miss Marova," they all said, and as Miss Marova took Lucy Jane's hand they added, "Goodbye, Lucy Jane."

As each person said "Goodbye," Lucy Jane's heart swelled with pride. Did they all know that their ballerina was taking her out to tea? And in case they didn't she announced happily, "We're off to the Hotel Savoy for tea, my aunt knows," and she walked on air along the corridor, following the great star.

At the stage door, old Dave gave Miss Marova a little bow and his dog gave a little yap. He wished her good health and said, "Look forward to seeing you tomorrow."

Then Lucy Jane and the ballerina set off together through Covent Garden. Tea at the Savoy! What would her mother and father think of that!

When they arrived at the hotel, the doorman said, "Good afternoon, Miss Marova, how nice to see you."

He touched his hat, gave a small nod and rushed to push the revolving doors for Miss Marova to enter. The ballerina glided around and into the hotel, leaving Lucy Jane standing outside, watching the magic doors swallow up her friend. Not daring to follow in case she got caught in the spinning glass monster, she waited anxiously outside. The doorman looked down at her.

"Missy, are you with Miss Marova?" he asked, seeing Lucy Jane staring forlornly at the doors.

"I was," Lucy Jane replied, gazing at the door moving round and round in front of her just like her mouse's exercise wheel.

"My mouse must be very clever," she said thoughtfully, "She can get into her wheel easily and it goes round *sideways*. I can't manage this wheel and I'm standing up."

The doorman took her hand and put her into the nearest section. Lucy Jane noticed the door was divided into four, like four quarters of a cake. She pushed the door round and ended up exactly where she began, outside the hotel. Miss Marova could just be seen standing on the other side in the

middle of the big lobby, looking for her.

"Rabbits," Lucy Jane said to herself as she felt the chance of having tea with the ballerina slipping away. "Rabbits, if my mice can do it, so can I." And again she entered the great wheel. This time she couldn't manage to stop it in time to get out. So after the doorman had watched her miserably walk round twice, each time missing the exit, he decided to put his foot in the door and help her escape. Luckily, it stopped facing the lobby, and Lucy Jane lurched out and rushed breathlessly over to Miss Marova.

"Just checking that the door worked properly," she puffed, rather red in the face. If it's this difficult to get into the hotel, she thought, whatever will tea be like?

In fact, the tea passed comparatively uneventfully. Silent waiters, endlessly smiling and hovering, waited to pour the tea and serve the scones. A piano in the middle of the room played songs that Lucy Jane did not know and could not sing and everyone spoke in whispers.

The sound of the piano tinkling and the teacups clinking was pierced by Lucy Jane's voice saying, "These sandwiches would be just the right size for my dolls." And she held up one of the tiny crustless finger-shaped slithers of bread and popped it into her mouth. The room fell silent and ladies in fur hats turned round to look at her.

When the waiter brought the cakes they called "pastries", they too looked very small, and Miss Marova told Lucy Jane,

"You should cut them with your fork."

Lucy Jane took the little fork in her hand and carefully brought it down on the pastry. Unfortunately, the fork slipped, the cake zoomed off the plate and landed on the floor by a little dog at the next table who immediately scooped it up and ate it.

"So sorry about that, Tati. Slippery cake."

Miss Marova laughed. The ladies looked round again. "Well, at least the dog's been fed!"

Lucy Jane laughed too but she was wishing that the dog hadn't been fed and that she had managed to eat her cake.

At the end of tea, *six* cakes later, two more of which had gone to the dog, the ballerina and the little girl made their way through Covent Garden.

"I feel much better after that lovely tea," the ballerina said, as they arrived at the theatre. "Much better. I shall go home now and rest and tomorrow at ten o'clock, I'll see you for your lesson."

Lucy Jane smiled.

"Maybe you can even watch a rehearsal," the dancer added with a twinkle. "Be good." Then she stepped into her car and was driven off.

5

A ballet lesson

Sarah decided to leave in good time so that she could cook her niece a nourishing meal and put her to bed early, so she tidied up the Wardrobe, while Lucy Jane examined the rows of beautiful dresses lining the walls. In Lucy Jane's mind, she could imagine herself dancing in every one of them. She saw herself flying across the stage on a wire, dressed in a pale green butterfly costume, and standing in the swans' carriage she had seen in the store 'prop' room. She would be wearing a white cygnet's ballet dress and be drawn across the lake by the *corps de ballet*. Then she saw herself dancing the polka, or banging a tambourine with fluttering ribbons as she danced the tarantella.

She imagined great dancers partnering her and important people applauding her. It was a day-dream of a most special kind and when she heard her aunt's voice saying, "Come on, Lucy, off we go for supper," she was brought back to reality with a jolt.

"Oh, Aunt Sarah, I've been dreaming such lovely thoughts. Really lovely ones."

"Come on now," her aunt said, not noticing the look in her niece's eyes and handing her a Pierrot's costume to carry. "Take this for me," and they set off down the stairs.

Each carrying a large bundle of costumes needing to be mended, they left the warm theatre and made their way across the road to Sarah's flat. All you could see of Lucy Jane was the Pierrot hat on her head and her two pigtails sticking out above the pile of Pierrot costumes in her arms. Her feet stepped carefully as she staggered across the road trying not to trip up on the costumes.

"Mind how you go, duckie," Dave called after her as they struggled to the other side of the street.

"Going to get an early night," Lucy Jane shouted back to him from beneath the clothes, proud that she now seemed to be part of the theatre.

Once they had settled in the flat, Sarah cooked a splendid meal of roast chicken, brown rice and vegetables, which they ate sitting at the kitchen table. Despite having four cakes at tea, Lucy Jane was very hungry and asked for a second helping of chicken, broccoli and carrots.

"I want to keep my strength up for my ballet lesson tomorrow," and putting her knife and fork together, she said, "That's why, now I've finished, I don't mind going straight to bed."

Sarah said that was an excellent idea and tucked up her little niece, all snug with her tickly-rug, for a good night's sleep.

As she lay in her comfy bed on the sofa, Lucy Jane could hear her aunt using the sewing machine in her bedroom next door. The faint sound of music on her aunt's radio came to her ears as she snuggled further under the covers to dream.

"Aunt Sarah's not bad," were her last thoughts as she drifted into a happy sleep and forgot the world until morning.

Lucy Jane woke early next morning, very excited at the thought that today she really was going to have her ballet lesson with Miss Marova. She had taken dancing lessons at school – but this lesson, as far as Lucy Jane was concerned, was the real thing. Once again she arrived at the stage door on the dot of ten o'clock and she was overjoyed to see that Tatiana was in good health and already at the Theatre waiting for her.

The ballet room was a huge hall under the stage used for ballet classes and rehearsals. It was brightly lit and Lucy Jane could see her reflection in all the floor to ceiling mirrors on the walls. There was a big red 'No Smoking' sign by the door and, at the height of Lucy Jane's chin, a wooden rail, to hold on to all around the room. There were no windows and the room was hot and stuffy.

As Lucy Jane raced to change into her new ballet clothes, she had visions of herself dancing in a white ballet dress, balancing effortlessly on one point and doing dozens of turns, without ever getting dizzy or falling down. But, when Tatiana took her to the barre and made her exercise neatly and slowly, Lucy Jane realised for the first time that learning ballet properly was not quite as easy as she had expected.

The first exercises Tatiana showed her were the five positions of the feet, and then they practised the plié. She had to bend her legs sideways so that her knees went over her toes. To do a good plié seemed to Lucy Jane to be rather awkward and difficult, but she so wanted to be good, not only to please her new teacher, but also to show her parents all she had learnt when she got home, so she carefully watched, listened and copied every-

thing Tatiana said and did. Apart from small beads of perspiration which gathered on the ballerina's forehead, the work seemed effortless to Tatiana. But Lucy Jane was feeling quite out of breath. And as her body became hotter, her tights and leotard clung to her skin and felt sticky and uncomfortable.

"Now plié down, two, three, up, two, three and nice straight knees!" Tati chanted in a sing-song voice, to make Lucy Jane feel as though they were moving to music; and thus they methodically continued to work. When the lesson was over, the ballerina told Lucy Jane, "You have worked very hard. I am most pleased with you. If you work, you can be very, very good. A beautiful little dancer one day."

Lucy Jane filled with pride and instead of going straight back upstairs to her aunt, she lingered by the door hoping that Tatiana would ask her if she wanted to stay and watch the class. But the ballerina was busy practising in front of the mirror, apparently unaware that Lucy Jane was still there. When everyone else arrived, they were also too busy changing or limbering up to notice her at all. Lucy Jane stood by the door, looking on longingly. When the ballet mistress appeared, she was amazed to see an unknown little girl waiting in the room.

"What on earth are you doing here? Who do

you belong to?" she asked.

"I'm Sarah Wardrobe's niece, and Miss Tatiana Marova's pupil," said Lucy Jane importantly. "She has just given me a lesson."

"That's good. So you're a dancer," said the ballet mistress. "You're one of us."

Lucy Jane smiled, she felt very pleased to be included, but somehow she still did not have the courage to ask if she could stay. However, the ballet mistress assumed that the little girl was there to watch the class, and said, "Come on in and close the door behind you."

"Thank you, I wanted to watch the practising, but I didn't like to ask," Lucy Jane said gratefully.

A ripple of laughter went round the room. Miss Marova looked up. She walked straight over to Lucy Jane, took her by the hand, and led her to the ballet mistress.

"Dotti darling, can Lucy Jane sit by the piano please?" she said, and without more ado, Lucy Jane was put on a chair beside the pianist, Miss Keep, and the class commenced.

The piano was rather old and tinny and sounded like a barrel-organ, but the pianist played with tremendous verve and Lucy Jane thoroughly enjoyed its sound ringing through her head. All during the class, which lasted an hour and twenty minutes, Lucy Jane's eyes were riveted on Tati who danced more beautifully than anyone else.

6

A surprise audition

The next week passed happily, with Lucy Jane taking a private ballet lesson every morning, and afterwards watching the class in the ballet room or a rehearsal from the stalls. There she sat, a lone figure in a sea of seats, watching the stage, her head bobbing from side to side in time to the music as everyone danced. In the afternoon, if her aunt had no other plans for her, she would practise by herself in the Wardrobe.

"Miss Marova says I'm coming on beautifully," Lucy Jane said happily. And it certainly looked to Sarah as if this was the case.

One morning, when Lucy Jane arrived for her lesson, she was surprised to find that Tati was not there, and instead, seven little girls in practice clothes dancing in front of the mirror. Lucy Jane was rather taken aback. Were they *all* going to have a lesson with Miss Marova? And if so, why hadn't Tatiana told her? She looked at the girls and said fearfully, "Are you supposed to be here?"

"Yes," said the tallest girl and gave Lucy a look as much as to say 'And are *you* supposed to be here?'

"We're auditioning at ten thirty," added the tall girl grandly.

"I see," said Lucy Jane, thinking perhaps it was today that Miss Marova had a matinée and was not going to give her a lesson. She stood nervously for a moment watching the girls dancing and asked quietly, "I'm sorry, what is auditioning?"

"It means trying out for a role you want to play on stage," the same tall girl answered in a bored fashion.

"I see," Lucy Jane said, then added hastily, "What role?"

"'The Nutcracker'."

"I'm sorry?" Lucy Jane had never heard of it.

"You know, the children in the 'Nutcracker'. Not much dancing really, but it's good experience to be on stage with this company. You know the ballet of course?"

Lucy Jane did not know, but she did not want to sound too ignorant, so she said nothing.

"They do 'The Nutcracker' every winter and the girls from the ballet school always audition for it," said the tall girl.

"Of course," said Lucy Jane knowingly, wondering all the time if Miss Marova knew anything about the girls auditioning. She had a strong feeling that she was not wanted in the room, so very reluctantly she started to go.

As she was leaving, Dotti, the ballet mistress, followed by Leonard Wallington, the choreographer, entered the room.

"Hello, Lucy Jane!" said Dotti.

The tall girl gave Lucy Jane a jealous look, then smiled at the choreographer.

"You'd better change quickly if you want to join the others," the ballet mistress continued, and without asking any questions, Lucy Jane changed her clothes.

While she was changing, Leonard Wallington lit a cigarette and put it in his black and gold cigarette holder. He was wearing a long, dark coat with a large black felt hat and a very long yellow scarf wound three times round his neck. As he sat down on the chair by the piano and drew on his cigarette, Lucy Jane looked at the big 'No Smoking' sign and then at his cigarette, but she decided it would be better to say nothing. The girls chatted and danced about while Dotti stood and talked to Leonard until Miss Keep, the pianist, arrived. Then Dotti clapped her hands and asked for "Quiet!"

"Now girls, this is Leonard Wallington, our choreographer, and Miss Keep, our pianist."

Miss Keep nodded her head to the girls, and to the choreographer who just carried on smoking.

Although Lucy Jane was completely ready she had no idea what she should do, or what was about to happen, so she kept well out of the way and pretended to be tying up the ribbons on her ballet shoe.

Then the choreographer rose from his chair and said in a slow tired voice, "Young ladies, first of all, just run round the room as freely and gracefully as you can, and pretend you're looking for something, or if you wish, for someone. Now

off you go – in time to the music," and he sat down again looking very bored.

"Easy!" said the tall girl, "We did this last year," and they all tripped off round the room at high speed, except Lucy Jane who decided to go at half time, as though she was slowly stalking a tiger. Dotti, the ballet mistress, amused, watched and murmured, "Lovely, very original," and even Leonard the choreographer perked up and looked quite interested. Then he drawled, "Stop, thank you girls," and everyone ground to a halt. He and Dotti stood at the side of the room and quietly chatted together. They looked as though they were talking deaf and dumb language with their hands as they made little signals with their fingers and wrists dancing. The choreographer turned to them and said, "Dotti is going to put a few steps

together for you and I'd like you all to learn them.
And when you've practised, dance them one by
one for me, in time to the music. The piano, as
you know, will be played by the lovely Miss Keep
here," and with a flourish he sat down, lit another
cigarette and again looked totally bored.

The ballet mistress showed the girls the steps
and they eagerly tried to copy her. Lucy Jane
found learning the little dance extremely hard,
and twice she tripped over her own feet as they
got tangled round each other.

Then the big moment came and each child was
asked to dance alone. The tall girl went first.

"Name?" asked the ballet mistress.

"Samantha Evans, of course," said the tall girl
as though everyone should know.

"Oh yes, I remember, you were here last year,"
said Dotti and jotted down her name on a piece of
paper.

Samantha gave everyone a superior smile and
began to dance.

"Very nice. Thank you, Samantha. Wait at the
side, please. Next!"

The next six girls danced almost perfectly as far
as Lucy Jane was concerned and suddenly, everyone had had a turn except Lucy Jane who,
although she rather hoped she had been forgotten,
was practising in the corner, in case she was not.

"Now you! The little one in the corner," the

choreographer drawled, looking straight at Lucy Jane. "You. Come on! Name?"

Lucy Jane turned round, startled. She had never been so frightened. The words "Now you! Name?" shot through her heart.

"Lucy Jane Tadworth," she said, her legs shaking and she wished with all her might she was not there. When Lucy Jane danced, she managed to forget most of the steps and the girls at the side of the room started to giggle. Although Lucy Jane made a terrible mess of her turn, the steps she invented were very pretty and certainly showed that Miss Marova's work had not been in vain. When she had finished, Leonard rose to his feet and looked at her thoughtfully for some time.

"Do you want to try again, young lady?"

"Why?" said Lucy Jane. The girls giggled.

"Because, my darling child, you didn't seem to get it quite right, did you?"

"I know," agreed Lucy Jane timidly, "But I don't think I can get it right even if I do do it again."

"Try!" he said imperiously.

So Lucy Jane had no option but to dance again.

This time she became quite carried away by Miss Keep's splendid pounding on the piano, she and the music seemed to belong together. Although she did not dance exactly the same steps she had been taught, her feet seemed to move neatly into place and her arms looked graceful and soft. The result was pleasing and when she had finished, Dotti and Leonard again went into a corner to discuss their candidates. All the girls waited in silence, biting their nails, and it seemed a considerable time later that Leonard glided into the middle of the room with a list of the girls' results.

"Now then," he pronounced, "I'd like to use you, Alice and you, Carole, and you three over there," he said, pointing to the first five of the girls who had danced and ignoring the tall Samantha Evans. Samantha let out a sulky sigh and announced disdainfully, looking straight at the choreographer, "It says 'No Smoking'," and she flounced past him.

The other girl who had not been chosen looked very disappointed, but Lucy Jane was relieved it was all over. Then suddenly the choreographer pointed straight at her and said, "We'll also keep our little 'personality turn', Lucy Jane, to understudy."

Lucy Jane had no idea what 'understudy' meant, but she hoped it did not mean 'trespassing'. In case it did, she felt she should explain why she was there.

"You see, I'm really only waiting for my lesson with Miss Marova," she said, hoping this would sort everything out.

"Ah! So Tati teaches you, does she?"

The great man became very interested as he looked down at the little girl.

"Great dancer and obviously a great teacher. Surprising. Good. All the more reason why you should understudy all five girls. If any of them are ill, you take their place and go on! You see, you'll have five chances of dancing instead of only one!"

Lucy Jane's mouth fell open. She had never imagined that anything like this would happen. She wondered if Tati had known there would be an audition and had deliberately left her to see how she would get on.

As Samantha Evans was packing her practice clothes, she turned to Lucy Jane and said, "Well, the one thing I'd hate to be is an understudy. You know what they say? Once an understudy, always an understudy," and she picked up her things and stalked grandly from the room.

The other little girls rushed over to Lucy Jane.

"Don't worry," one of them said, "It's jolly good to be chosen to understudy – especially if you've never auditioned before."

"I'm jolly glad Samantha wasn't chosen to play one of the mice," another one said as they crowded closer to Lucy Jane.

"It's all right," Lucy Jane said, "I don't mind. You see, I didn't even know what an 'underthing' was until a moment ago. I'm only here because

82

my Mummy's having a baby."

"Do you really have lessons with Miss Marova?" asked Alice.

"Yes," Lucy Jane confirmed proudly, then she shyly admitted, "I'm sorry, I can't remember any of your names."

"I'm Alice, and she's Carole," Alice said pointing to the dark-haired girl, "and we call her Roly Poly," she said, touching the middle girl's tummy. "It's only a nickname of course, but she just loves eating swiss rolls! These two are the twins, Celia and Maria."

The girls all laughed and Lucy Jane felt warm inside and relieved that everyone was so friendly.

"Now, now, girls, you had better change and go home and Lucy Jane, you had better go upstairs to your aunt," said Dotti.

"What? Does your aunt work here?" asked Roly Poly enviously.

"Yes, she's the wardrobe mistress."

"Ooh!"

There was an awed silence.

"You know Miss Marova *and* the wardrobe mistress!" Lucy Jane nodded. The girls looked at each other with a look that said 'She must be really special', then they started to get ready.

When Lucy Jane had changed, she rushed upstairs to find her Aunt Sarah.

"Guess what?" she said breathlessly to Sarah as she arrived at the Wardrobe. "I'm in the Nut ballet."

"What?" her aunt answered disbelievingly.

"Yes! I'm there just in case and I'm not playing a mouse!" and she waved her arms and danced about the room. "I shall have to practise every day."

"Rehearse," her aunt corrected her.

"Rehearse every day for the Nut ballet."

"'The Nutcracker'."

"And if someone's ill, I'll be the undertaker."

"Understudy," her aunt said.

"Oh, it's so lovely, Aunt Sarah!" and she continued to dance. Suddenly, there was a loud knock at the door and Lucy Jane immediately wanted to jump into the skip. The door opened and a fireman strolled into the room. Lucy Jane rushed to the rails of clothes and slid between some ballet dresses hanging there.

"Hello there. I'm doing my rounds, just check-ing before the matinée," and he sauntered round the room looking at all the electric plugs.

"I hear you've got your niece staying,"

"Yes," said Sarah and carried on sorting out the tights. "She's going to be an understudy in the 'Nutcracker', she's here somewhere."

"Well, make sure she's not in the theatre with-out permission during performances."

"Of course," replied Sarah. "I got permission for her to be here the day she arrived."

"Got a cup of tea brewing, by any chance?" the fireman asked suddenly.

"Just a quick cup," Sarah said and she turned on the kettle. The fireman sat chatting and drinking his tea for what seemed like hours to Lucy Jane. She didn't know whether she should stay hidden or not, so she remained behind the clothes hoping that she was doing the right thing.

Finally, Sarah said to the fireman, "Off you go, you can't stay and chat any longer. I've too much to do for the Royal Gala next week. I must get on with my work."

The fireman downed his tea and strode off cheerily. Lucy Jane was pleased to see him go because the only thing she wanted to do was talk to Tatiana about being an understudy.

"Let's go and tell Miss Marova what's happened to me," she said and looked pleadingly at her aunt.

"There's a matinée today, Lucy darling, I don't really think we should disturb her."

"Please," Lucy Jane pleaded. "Please."

Sarah thought for a moment.

"Well, I suppose you could ring her," she said, relenting.

"Hurray!" shouted Lucy Jane and rushed to the telephone.

"Can I speak to Miss Marova please?"

She waited excitedly for the ballerina to answer. At last she heard Tatiana's soft voice say, "Hallo?"

"Tati, I'm going to be an understudy in 'The Nutcracker'."

A moment later when Lucy Jane put down the receiver, she announced excitedly to her aunt, "Tati says I can go down and see her," and so saying, she dashed to the door.

"Wait a moment, wait a moment!" Sarah said and she proceeded to wrap Lucy Jane up in a ballet dress.

"What are you doing?" squeaked Lucy Jane, amazed to find herself in her aunt's arms.

"We'll give Miss Marova a surprise and make it look as if I'm carrying a ballet dress downstairs and not you!"

"And I'll be inside?" Lucy Jane inquired.

"Yes," laughed her aunt.

"How lovely! Let's go!" and they set off.

The first person they saw on the stairs was the fireman.

"Taking Miss Marova her clothes?" he asked.

"That's right," answered Sarah, smiling to her-self, and she hurried down the stairs with Lucy Jane hanging inside the dress like a giggling rag doll.

When Sarah arrived in Miss Marova's dressing room, Lucy Jane jumped out of the dress and appeared before the ballerina as if by magic. Tatiana looked exceedingly surprised.

"I'm going to be in 'The Nutcracker' if someone's ill. Lovely! Lovely!" and she bounced around the room overjoyed at the thought that she might have the chance to go on stage. "And it's all because I've learnt to dance. Thank you for teaching me, Tati."

The ballerina was smiling, thrilled to see her pupil so happy. She stopped putting on her make-up and knelt down beside Lucy Jane.

"Now, if you're going to be an understudy, you're really going to have to work hard in case you do go on stage. You need to dance with beautiful stretched feet, a straight back and graceful arms. No thumbs sticking out!"

The ballerina demonstrated what she meant and again added, "Hard work, Lucy Jane. Lots of hard work."

Hard work sounded like beautiful words to Lucy Jane at that moment.

"Good. I *love* hard work," she said, "when it's work I like and I don't find it too hard."

When Tati had given Lucy Jane a kiss and wished her good luck, Sarah led her quickly back upstairs. Lucy Jane wanted to telephone her mother in hospital.

Mrs Tadworth was surprised to hear Lucy Jane's voice and delighted to hear her enthusiastic account of her days at the theatre.

"I'm so glad you're happy, Lucy darling," she said. "You see, we knew that you would love staying with Sarah. Daddy told you that the theatre was a magic place, and now you know it is."

Lucy Jane nodded. She was so happy to talk to her mother. She had often thought about her but somehow it had never been the right time to telephone her.

"You know, Mummy, I nearly forgot to ask about Tilly," then without waiting for news of her kitten, Lucy Jane went on breathlessly, "I went through a sort of mouse door at a hotel when Miss Marova took me to tea."

Mrs Tadworth only managed to repeat the words "mouse door?" before her daughter interrupted, "Are you rested enough to have the baby yet?"

"Not quite, darling, the doctor says he wants me to rest for a few more days before the baby is born. But it won't be long now."

"Oh good," said Lucy Jane. "Sarah says The Royal Nutcracker will be in about two weeks so you can come and see it. But I may not go on stage. I'm only an understudy."

"Well, we'll see," said Mrs Tadworth kindly.

Then they blew kisses and said goodbye.

"Aunt Sarah," Lucy Jane shouted to her aunt who was standing by the ironing board, "I think the baby will be born soon so maybe Mummy can come to The Royal Nutcracker."

Lucy Jane was feeling very happy. Everything seemed to be going her way.

7

Getting ready for the First Night

Lucy Jane and her new friends Alice, Carole, Celia, Maria and Roly Poly spent the next few days having a ballet class each morning, followed by a rehearsal.

Some days the girls practised in the big rehearsal room under the stage. Because the children were under sixteen, they were not allowed to work more than a few hours each day. So every other day they practised for an hour in the morning, and then they all rested for a while and ate their packed sandwich lunches, sitting in a little circle on the floor, sharing food and chatting nonstop.

In the afternoons they would rehearse once more. One of the things Lucy Jane and her new friends enjoyed most was watching all the other dancers rehearse. They were friendly and kind to the children. One of the dancers gave them her last six glucose sweets and shared her orange with them. "Only five more days to go until the opening," she said happily.

Then she popped the last segment of orange into her mouth and pretended to be very nervous and knocked her knees together to make the girls laugh.

It was lovely for Lucy Jane to have young friends in the theatre, and sometimes when Sarah was particularly busy and if the children were not needed, one of the girls would invite Lucy Jane home for lunch or tea. The whole stay had been full of delights and surprises. Lucy Jane's happiness was a great relief to Mrs Tadworth, who had stayed in hospital longer than originally expected. When Lucy Jane thought of all the fuss she had made about going to stay with her Aunt Sarah, she felt ashamed. Now she thought the theatre was one of the most wonderful and exciting places in the world.

The day of the dress rehearsal was filled with a magic all of its own, and although Lucy Jane was not allowed to dance or rehearse because none of the girls were ill, she felt a lovely feeling inside. The theatre buzzed with all the excitement and activity of a family getting ready for Christmas.

The dancers of the *corps de ballet* were very helpful and showed the children where to enter the stage, where to rub their feet in the rosin tray so that their ballet shoes would not slip as they danced on stage, and made sure that they did not have stage fright. But as it was a Sunday, the children were not allowed to work for very long so they had to go home as soon as they had done one rehearsal in costume. Lucy Jane was the exception. Because she was Sarah's niece, she was allowed to stay up all evening and watch the big dress rehearsal with the full orchestra. Sarah was busy back-stage so Dotti took care of Lucy Jane and they sat in the stalls together, watching Miss Marova's Sugar Plum Fairy solo, and the rest of the ballet. Sometimes the lights or scenery or orchestra were not exactly as they should be, so Leonard the choreographer would scream "Sto-o-p!" from the stalls and everything and everyone would grind to a halt while the problem was sorted out.

Lucy Jane wished that she too could be up on the stage dancing but each time she was about to go off into a little daydream of her own, Leonard's voice would be heard screaming to someone and Dotti would have to jump to her feet and rush over to calm him, and help get the dress rehearsal started again.

The next day was the first performance of 'The Nutcracker' and everyone was frantically rushing about. There were all sorts of last minute errands, the children suddenly needed more hairclips and the men ran out of body make-up. Sarah did her best to keep calm in all the pandemonium.

The girls' dressing room was right at the top of the building, unlike Miss Marova's which was near the stage. It was painted in shiny cream paint and looked very large and bare, with ten mirrors and dressing tables and ten old wooden chairs round the side of the room. There were no flowers or greetings cards or any of the colourful items that made the ballerina's dressing room look so pretty.

Quite naturally, Lucy Jane was feeling rather left out. No one was ill, so she knew she was not

going to be in the ballet. She watched enviously as the girls put a little rouge on their cheeks and tied ribbons in their hair. She had been given a costume to wear 'just in case' but as all five girls had arrived at the theatre, there was no chance of her having to put it on.

She tried to be a good sport, but all she really wanted to do was hide away in the dressing room and cry. But she did not want to let the side down, so she made a great effort to help the girls change. She brushed their hair and told them how pretty they looked.

The orchestra could be heard tuning up and faint strands of music drifted up the stairs. The children were all dressed and ready and the chaperone, Mrs Stone, who was in charge of the children, sat on the only large and comfortable dressing room armchair, drinking endless cups of tea from her thermos. She was knitting a candy pink dress for her grand-daughter.

Suddenly an announcement came over the loudspeaker: "Beginners, Act I, please!" and a flurry of nerves and excitement passed through the dressing room.

As Alice skipped around excitedly waiting to go down, she said, "Wear your dress anyway, Lucy, just for the fun of dressing up, and then it will seem as if we're all going on stage."

Lucy Jane thought this was a lovely idea, so while her friends practised in the corner, she put on her costume. Then they all huddled in a circle complaining of butterflies in their tummies and chanting, "I'm glad I'm not playing one of the mice in 'The Nutcracker'."

Mrs Stone told all the girls except Lucy Jane to go and wait at the side of the stage. So poor Lucy Jane sat quietly alone, longing to join them. She could hear the overture playing, the chaperone's knitting needles clicking and her own feet scratching on the bar across her chair. She was just wondering if she dare put some make-up on her cheeks when suddenly there was a loud knock at the door and the stage door-keeper's voice shouted, "Lucy Jane – something for you."

Lucy Jane rushed to the door and took a large white envelope from his hand. She was so excited, she could hardly tear it open. Inside was a card from Tati. It read, 'To my clever little pupil. I'm sorry you won't be dancing today. Maybe another day. Lots of love. Tati and Miss Soft-paws.'

Lucy Jane kissed the card, pushed it down the front of her dress and rushed towards the door. Mrs Stone dropped her knitting and called, "Where are you going?"

"Downstairs to thank Miss Marova for her card, Mrs Stone."

The chaperone obviously thought that Lucy Jane had no right to be talking to the star and told her to come back at once and sit down, which Lucy Jane obediently did, cursing under her breath.

"Rats and rabbits," Lucy Jane whispered as she folded her arms and plonked herself in the nearest chair. She sat swinging her legs and longing to be out of the old dragon's sight. All she wanted was to be at the side of the stage with the other girls, where she could thank Tatiana for the card, and feel part of the whole event.

Suddenly, outside the dressing room door,

there was a tremendous commotion. Lucy Jane nervously jumped to her feet. She felt sure, judging by the high-pitched frenzy coming from the stairs, that there must be a fire. She rushed over to Mrs Stone and told her to get her handbag, at which point the door swung open and a breathless, dishevelled Company Manager hurled himself in the room and grabbed Lucy Jane by the arm. "Quick, Lucy Jane, run," he panted.

"I think it's a fire, Mrs Stone, come on. Fire!" Lucy Jane shouted, and they both ran towards the stairs. The Company Manager anxiously ushered Lucy Jane down first, and Mrs Stone tried to follow, clutching her handbag. Then the Company Manager yelled to Lucy Jane, "You're on, you're on. If you don't hurry, you'll be off!"

Lucy Jane had no idea what he meant but she tried to keep up with him as he overtook her and galloped down the steps two at a time. He dragged her through the pass door and into the wings saying, "Go on, Alice has just sprained her ankle. Quick, you're on!"

Lucy Jane had no time to be frightened or ask about her friend. She could hear her music so she ran on stage. As she danced into the limelight, everyone crowded into the wings to watch her.

"She's taking her part beautifully," said Lillie, dabbing her eyes with her handkerchief.

The little dancing Lucy Jane had to do, she did

perfectly, but, towards the end, there was a soft clattering noise as Miss Marova's card fluttered from Lucy Jane's dress and sailed to the floor. At first, Lucy Jane could not imagine what it was, but she managed to bend down and pick it up in time to the music making the whole movement look like a graceful curtsy, and then she pushed it back into the bodice of her dress.

On the other side of the stage Miss Marova stood watching with tears in her eyes – she was so proud to see her little pupil taking over so perfectly and moreover, making the accident of the card falling from her dress look as though it was part of the ballet. As the girls came off stage, Miss Marova hugged them all and gave Lucy Jane a special squeeze.

"Bravo, bravo, my little Lucy Jane!" and so saying she kissed her on both cheeks.

"Oh, wasn't it awful about the card?" said Lucy Jane, absolutely ashamed. "I wanted to keep it near me, so I had it tucked in my dress – but I didn't know then that I was going to have a chance to dance."

Sarah, who was also in the wings, told her niece not to worry. "You did very well, darling, I'm very proud of you," she whispered. "No more hiding in skips for you. Now, if the fireman comes in, you can tell him 'I am *in* the ballet!'" and she hugged her niece and ushered her back to the Wardrobe. On the way upstairs they found Mrs Stone on the landing holding her handbag and saying, "I can't smell a fire."

Lucy Jane shouted to her as she passed, "Mrs Stone I've been 'on', I've been on stage, Mrs Stone," but she was too exhilarated to stop and explain, she just added "I'm sorry, Mrs Stone, false alarm, no fire," and continued to rush upstairs to telephone her mother and father and tell them her exciting news.

"Guess what, Daddy?" Lucy Jane said ecstatically to her father on the telephone, "I've just danced on stage in the ballet. Alice broke her foot or something and . . ." she stopped abruptly. "Oh heavens" she said, suddenly remembering her friend. "Poor Alice! I'd better go, Daddy, I must see her. And, oh, Daddy" she added as she was about to leave, "Is there a baby yet?"

But without waiting for a reply to her first question she asked another and another, "If I dance again on Thursday in The Royal Nut-cracker, can you and Mummy come and see me? Oh, yes, and can you bring my autograph book and a present for Miss Marova?"

Her father could hardly answer all these questions at once, so he started with the news of the new baby. "You've got a little brother, Lucy, so you can come home soon. The baby suddenly arrived last night and Mummy is fine so she will be out of the hospital on Wednesday and I expect she will be well enough to come to the ballet."

"Yippee" shouted Lucy Jane.

"You seem to be having a wonderful time, darling, but please can I have a word with your aunt?"

Lucy Jane said goodbye and handed the receiver to Sarah and while her aunt reassured her father that Lucy Jane was well and happy, she rushed off to find Alice.

When she arrived, Alice was sitting in their big dressing room with her foot in a red fire bucket filled with icy water. Mrs Stone was holding her hand and saying dolefully, "This should never have happened – those stairs are a danger. A real danger. What will her mother say?"

Lucy Jane rushed over to Alice and put her arm round her friend. "Poor Alice," she said.

"I hear you were wonderfully good, Lucy," Alice said bravely.

"Oh Alice!" Lucy Jane fought back the tears. "I'd much rather that you hadn't fallen down and that *you* could have gone on."

The girls looked at each other consolingly.

"Guess what?" Alice said, abruptly changing the subject. "Do you know who brought me upstairs?"

Lucy Jane thought for a moment. "One of the dancers?" she asked.

"No," cried Alice joyfully. "The Company Manager! He carried me all the way here!" The two girls started to laugh happily.

"Ow!" squealed Alice. "My foot just touched the side of the bucket." And she screwed up her face in pain.

Lucy Jane looked worried.

"My parents are coming in a minute but I won't be able to walk for days. I'll definitely miss the Royal Performance."

As Alice spoke, tears filled her eyes and Lucy Jane felt rather ashamed of all the happiness she had enjoyed in going on stage in Alice's place. It looked as if she would be dancing at the Royal Gala Performance on Thursday after all, which meant her parents would be able to see her. She didn't know whether she should feel overjoyed for herself, or upset for Alice. She managed to feel both.

"You know something, Alice?" Lucy Jane said sweetly. "You've been a real friend to me and now you've let me dance. Thank you."

The two girls hugged each other and Lucy Jane ran from the room.

When she returned to the Wardrobe, Sarah was ironing Miss Marova's dress.

"What did Daddy say?" Lucy Jane asked breathlessly. "Can he and Mummy really come? Am I dancing again tonight? And is it really true that the Queen and her family are coming to see us dance next Thursday?"

"First," said Sarah, "We'll sit down and have some tea, and then I'll answer all your questions."

So Lucy Jane had no option but to be patient while her aunt prepared the food. To hurry the tea-making along, Lucy Jane said, "Let me put the butter on the bread," which she did. The waiting time seemed to speed by as she battled with the bread and butter, her knife, the plate, and her fingers. After much finger licking and picking up of broken bits of bread from the floor, the tea was finally ready.

They sat down and ate the brown bread, butter and honey, and some cheese and apple. Sarah poured herself a cup of tea and gave Lucy Jane a glass of fruit juice.

"Now, Lucy," she said, passing her niece the biscuits, "Firstly, yes, you are dancing again tonight and your Daddy is going to come and sit at the back of the Dress Circle to watch you. Secondly, yes, there is a Royal Performance next Thursday and the Royal Family are coming. I *think* your parents are coming too. Next, you must make a card and we'll send some flowers to your Mummy and the baby and, lastly, you must have a rest before tonight's performance."

Lucy Jane drew a card for her mother and new baby brother, while Sarah made her a little bed by pushing together two very old armchairs in the Wardrobe.

"Hop in," said Sarah. She covered her niece with a cloak so that she could rest before she went back on stage. Sarah always had a lot of work to do after the matinée preparing the costumes for the evening's performance. Although she had Lillie, and the other dressers to help her, it was a great rush so she was glad to see that Lucy Jane had fallen asleep at once. Now she could give all her time to the clothes that needed to be ironed or sewn before seven o'clock.

8

The Royal Gala Performance

That evening's performance was a very happy event for Lucy Jane. For the first time, she felt as though she was a real dancer going on stage as she sat quietly at her dressing table carefully brushing pink on her cheeks, and placing the ribbons in her hair. She had a sense of really belonging in the theatre. This was her first proper performance – she was part of the company, and in her heart she felt very excited and proud.

"I'm a dancer," she said to herself as she neatly tied up the ribbons on her ballet shoes. She waited silently with the other girls for Mrs Stone to tell them they could go downstairs.

"Don't be nervous," Roly Poly said. "We all think you're very good." Then at Mrs Stone's request they clasped hands and went downstairs in pairs.

Lucy Jane danced very well. No greetings card fell from her dress this time and the only mistake she made was running off stage the wrong way and bumping into the dancers just about to come on. This made the audience laugh and the Company Manager very cross. Immediately he strode round to see her.

"Lucy Jane, please come in early for a special rehearsal tomorrow to practise your exits and entrances," he said firmly.

"Sorry about that mistake," Lucy Jane replied sheepishly. "I got muddled with my left and right."

"Never let it happen again." The Company Manager looked very fierce. "I know you are only an understudy and younger than the other girls, and also have not rehearsed as much, but, when in doubt, follow them."

He had taken rather a hard line considering she had gone on at a moment's notice without any extra rehearsals but he was not used to dealing with children and treated Lucy Jane exactly as though she were an adult member of the company. He walked away leaving her standing at the side of the stage feeling hurt and bewildered. Then he suddenly stopped. Regretting his harsh action, he turned back towards her.

"Lucy Jane," he said kindly. "I didn't mean to be angry. You've done so well and we all think you are very good . . ." he paused. It seemed as though he wanted to say more but didn't know what to say, so he just repeated the word "good, yes, so good," and patted her hand and strode away, scratching his head.

Lucy Jane stood for a moment feeling a mixture of happiness and indignation, then she ran off to find her friends in the dressing room at the top of the theatre. Mrs Stone was waiting for her at the dressing room door.

"Why didn't you come upstairs with the others?" she asked anxiously. "I've been worried sick these last five minutes as to where you were."

There was a silence and Lucy Jane said nothing.

"I couldn't finish knitting this sleeve because of worrying about you. All the other girls are changed, ready to go home," Mrs Stone continued.

There was another silence and Lucy Jane felt that everything was very unfair. But she knew she must not be cheeky to Mrs Stone so she said quietly, "Mrs Stone, I'm so sorry you've been worried and couldn't finish knitting the sleeve, but I'm afraid the Company Manager kept me."

She hoped Mrs Stone would think the Company Manager had been congratulating her.

"I don't want this to happen again," Mrs Stone said sternly. At that moment, there was a knock at the door and to Lucy Jane's surprise Mr Tadworth popped his head round the door.

"Daddy!" cried Lucy Jane as she rushed into his

arms. "Daddy, I forgot you were coming."

Mr Tadworth hugged his daughter.

"Lucy Jane, it was lovely to see you dance and you were so good, all of you." He looked at the girls and then hugged his daughter again. "Change your clothes and come up to Sarah," he said, walking to the door.

"Oh, Mr Tadworth," Mrs Stone said, rushing over to catch him before he left. "I was just saying how good your little Lucy Jane is, considering she was only an understudy until this afternoon."

All the girls looked at each other and smiled, knowing Mrs Stone had been saying nothing of the sort. Lucy Jane giggled happily.

"I'm so pleased my Daddy's here. Isn't it exciting," she said. "See you tomorrow. Goodbye Mrs Stone." And she skipped off.

The day before the Royal Performance Lucy Jane was anxiously waiting to hear if her mother was feeling well enough to come and see her dance. All the other children's parents had been to see them perform at least twice so Lucy Jane was longing to be able to tell her friends that both her father and mother were going to come.

On the morning of the big day Sarah was sewing some sequins on a ballet dress in the Wardrobe when the telephone rang. Lucy Jane raced to pick up the receiver before her aunt. When she heard her father's voice, her heart began to leap about in her chest and she felt butterflies in her stomach but she couldn't say a word. She just clasped the telephone to her ear as her father's voice called "Hallo! Hallo! Is that you Sarah?"

"No, it's me," Lucy Jane answered at last. "Are you and Mummy coming to the Royal Gala Performance tonight?"

"Yes," her father replied. "Yes, both Mummy and I are coming, and we are taking you home afterwards."

Lucy Jane was so thrilled that she immediately dropped the receiver and bounced over to her aunt.

"They are coming tonight!" she cried and started to turn round happily in the middle of the room. Sarah smiled and replaced the receiver.

All the activity and preparation in the theatre on the evening of the Royal Performance seemed to Lucy Jane even more exciting than on any other day. The foyer and the stairways had been decorated with greenery, pine cones and ribbons, and the air smelt of gingerbread and Christmas.

Huge bouquets and arrangements of flowers tied with coloured satin ribbons kept arriving at the stage door. There were even five small baskets of flowers for each of the girls. Dave carried all the baskets up to the dressing room himself followed by his dog who was wearing a red ribbon from one of Miss Marova's bouquets.

"Well, duckies, you're all stars for a day," he said as he plonked the baskets of flowers on the dressing tables.

The children rushed to see who had sent them their flowers. They opened their cards and each one had the same message: 'Lots of love from a special admirer.'

Great excitement buzzed around the dressing room. Who could possibly be their secret admirer? Leonard, the choreographer? Dotti, the ballet mistress? Mrs Stone, the chaperone? No! Miss Marova? Could it be Miss Marova! The Company Manager? Or Sarah? Lucy Jane thought maybe it was her father. But the thrilling thing was, nobody knew.

As they dressed in their costumes for the first act, they could hear the orchestra tuning up over the loudspeaker. Then Leonard's voice boomed over the music.

"Royal Show tonight, darlings – give it your all. Be magnificent, girls." There was a short pause then he added, "Be magnificent, darling boys as well."

Silence. Everyone was quiet. Suddenly there was a roll of drums and the orchestra played *God Save The Queen*.

"The Queen and all the Royal Family are here!" whispered Carole.

"And my parents," added Lucy Jane.

And then they all rushed down the stairs to go on.

To everyone's happiness the Royal Performance went perfectly.

Mr and Mrs Tadworth sat proudly watching their daughter dance without making a single mistake. Because her parents were there, Lucy Jane felt quite frightened for the first time. She forgot the fact that the Queen and all her family were in the audience, and kept thinking she must be good to please her mother and father.

As Lucy Jane danced, something absolutely new and wonderful happened to her. She experienced an overwhelming love for ballet and for the sensation she felt as she danced her heart out on the great London stage. The beautiful music, the lights, the space, the limelight, the sound of the audience's applause, all added up to a magic feeling inside. Lucy Jane's mind and heart filled with a heady joy she knew she would remember all her life.

After the show all the artists including the children were told to wait back-stage in their costumes as the Royal Party were coming round to meet all the dancers. Everyone was going to be presented to them. Each of the small girls was given a small posy of sweet-smelling flowers called freesias, to give to the different ladies in the Royal Party.

The Royal Party arrived. The children waited until they were given a signal by the Company Manager to step forward and present them. As it happened, Lucy Jane had to present her posy to the pretty young woman who had been sitting in the box watching the ballet the day Lucy Jane arrived and got lost.

As she handed over the posy, all the photographers clustered round Lucy Jane, the smallest member of the Company, and took photographs.

"I've seen you here before," the lovely young woman said as Lucy Jane stepped forward.

"Yes," Lucy Jane replied as she curtsied. "And I've seen you too." Everyone laughed and smiled. When the Royal Party had spoken to all the dancers, they drifted out of sight and were taken on a tour to see the scenery and the whole of the back-stage by the Company Manager. Then Lucy Jane rushed over to Miss Marova.

"Tati, my Mummy and Daddy are here tonight. Can they come and speak to you?"

Tati took Lucy Jane by the hand and said of course they could. So it was arranged that Mr and Mrs Tadworth would go and meet Miss Marova in her dressing room when Lucy Jane was ready to go home.

Miss Marova was sitting at her dressing table with her crochet shawl wrapped around her shoulders when Mr and Mrs Tadworth knocked at the door. Lucy Jane stood between her mother and father, holding their hands and beaming happily up at them, her cheeks very pink from all the excitement. It was lovely to have her parents with her, and to introduce them to Miss Marova who had been so kind to her.

"She's a lovely little dancer," Miss Marova said as she greeted the Tadworth family. "Lovely, and I'd be happy to give her lessons when I am not too busy." She paused and smiled, then added, "As long as she practises hard and works well at school and in her ballet lessons."

Lucy Jane had never imagined that Tati would suggest anything so lovely and she waited anxiously for her parents' reply.

Mr Tadworth said nothing and Lucy Jane thought that perhaps they didn't like the idea, but at last Mrs Tadworth said shyly, "This is so kind, Miss Marova. I don't know what to say." And she looked down and blushed before starting again, "I know Lucy would be thrilled to have a lesson with you when you are not too busy. She has been so happy here and she admires you so very much and we too would be happy and honoured . . ." Mrs Tadworth stopped and looked down again.

Everyone nodded and smiled. It was time to go home. The Tadworths said goodbye to Tati and Sarah and Lillie and all the other members of the Company. As they were leaving, they bumped into a party of smartly dressed people on their way to Miss Marova's dressing room. The men were in dinner jackets and the women wore long dresses. One of them was holding a bottle of champagne.

"We've come to toast our darling Tati, the greatest ballerina," they called as they walked in. The Tadworths slipped away quietly.

Lucy Jane slept on her mother's lap all the way

home in the car. She didn't even wake up when her parents tucked her up in her own little bedroom. Nor did she hear her kitten, Tilly, jump onto the bed and settle down at her feet.

The next morning Lucy Jane woke to find her mother leaning over her bed.

"Lucy darling, we've got two surprises for you!"

Lucy Jane opened her eyes and saw her mother's smiling face looking down at her. She put her arms up to wrap them round her mother's neck, when she saw, for the first time, her new brother.

"Oh, Mummy! The new baby!" Lucy Jane cried excitedly.

"Yes, darling. Look, he's your own little brother," and she lowered the baby so that Lucy Jane could kiss him.

"And this is the second surprise," Mr Tadworth said, suddenly appearing from behind his wife. He pushed a newspaper into Lucy Jane's hand. On the front page was a picture of Lucy Jane in her ballet costume, curtseying to present her flowers. Above the picture were the words, 'Youngest ballet star meets Royal Star at the Christmas Gala!'

"It's me!" Lucy Jane exclaimed as she looked at the picture. "It's me and the lady in the silk dress."

"Yes, it's you," Mr Tadworth said and lifted his daughter out of bed. "It's you, the youngest little star. And now our youngest little star can help me decorate the Christmas tree."

Christmas was especially wonderful for Lucy Jane that year, for not only was she home with her new baby brother, but Sarah, Miss Marova and Miss Softpaws all came to join the Tadworths' Christmas gathering.

It was such a happy day. When they'd eaten the Christmas pudding and pulled all the crackers, Miss Marova raised her glass and toasted everyone.

"I have never enjoyed a Christmas so much and I am so happy to have the lovely Tadworth family and little Lucy Jane as my new friends." And she handed Lucy Jane something all wrapped up in white tissue paper.

Inside Lucy Jane found a pair of Tati's own pink satin point shoes. Lucy Jane went pink with pleasure. Later, as Lucy Jane sat on the sofa with her mother and Tati, holding the ballet shoes on her lap, she smiled up at her father and Sarah standing by the fire.

"I'm so glad, Daddy, you have a sister like Aunt Sarah," she said, beaming at Sarah, "Otherwise I would never have had such a lovely adventure at the theatre and been able to dance in a real ballet."

With that, she did her special trick of suddenly falling asleep. Surrounded by all the people she loved most, her head fell onto her mother's shoulder and she slept and dreamed of all the wonderful ballet lessons and performances to come.

Glossary

Audition Singing, dancing or acting for the Director of a play, musical or ballet, when trying to get a part.

Auditorium The half of the theatre in which the audience sits to watch the show.

Backcloth Huge canvas cloth that covers the whole of the back of the stage, often with trees, or sky, or sea painted on it, which makes the background to the production.

Back-stage The part of the theatre which is used for dressing rooms, prop rooms, rehearsal rooms, the Wardrobe and the costume store.

Ballerina Star female dancer.

Ballet master or mistress
The person in charge of teaching
and rehearsing the *corps de ballet*.

Barre Round wooden rail, waist-high to an adult, which dancers hold on to whilst practising their exercises.

120

Ballet   There are many ballets but these are four of the most popular:

Swan Lake   The story of a prince who falls in love with a princess who has been turned into a swan by a wicked magician called Von Rotbart.
(Music by Tchaikovsky)

Sleeping Beauty   The story of a princess who has had a spell cast upon her by a wicked fairy who was angry because she was not invited to the christening. She is doomed to die at the age of sixteen but the Lilac Fairy casts another spell so that the princess will not die, but sleep for a hundred years and be woken by a prince.
(Music by Tchaikovsky)

Giselle   The story of a peasant girl who falls in love with a prince who pretends to be a peasant. Unfortunately, the prince has already promised to marry a princess and so the peasant girl dies of a broken heart.
(Music by Adolphe Adam)

Nutcracker   The story of a little girl called Clara and her adventures in a magic toy shop.
(Music by Tchaikovsky)

Ballet Shoes   Soft satin or soft leather shoes – the type usually worn by little girls when they first start to dance. Point shoes – shoes which have hard toes and in which dancers do 'point work' – dance on their toes.

Character shoes – leather shoes with a 1½″ (38 mm) heel and a strap across the instep; worn for Spanish, or similar, dancing.

Chaperone The person who looks after young performers under the age of 16 while they are in the theatre or at the television studio. The chaperone often supervises school work too, if the child is missing school on account of the engagement.

Choreographer The man or woman who puts together the steps of a dance or ballet.

Company Manager The man or woman in charge of all the artists while they are in the theatre, paying their wages, sending for the doctor if they are hurt and making sure that everything runs smoothly behind the scenes.

Corps de ballet The dancers that form the background or chorus of a ballet.

Cue The piece of music or word which is the signal for a dancer or actor to start to dance or speak.

Dress rehearsal The final rehearsal before the opening night when, for the first time, the performers wear the costumes that they will be wearing in the show, with full lights and scenery and the full orchestra playing.

Dresser The lady, or man, who looks after the costumes of a performer during the show. Dressers often also make the tea, tidy the dressing table, and run errands.

Dressing rooms The rooms back-stage where the performers change and get ready to go on stage.

Encore A French word meaning again. When the performers receive so much applause that the audience wants them to perform again, they do an encore.

Fittings Trying on costumes to be worn in a show so that the dressmaker can check that the hem is the right length, the waist is the right size and that everything is perfect for the performance.

Position One   *Position Two*   *Position Three*

Position Four   *Position Five*

Footlights The lights that run along the floor at the front of the stage. In the old days, these were not electric lights but candles.

'The Green' Dancers' and actors' name for the stage.

Leg warmers Woolly stockings, without feet, that come to the knee and keep the muscles of the leg warm so that the dancer doesn't get stiff after practising.

Leotard A practice garment like a one-piece swimsuit that dancers wear for a ballet class.

Lighting box The room from which all the light switches for the show are operated.

Limbering up Exercises to warm up the muscles in preparation for dancing.

Matinée Afternoon show.

On point Standing on your toes in point shoes.

Orchestra A group of musicians who play music.

Pass door The door that goes between the back-stage area where all the artists are, into the auditorium where the audience sits.

Pigs' Ears You should never have 'pigs' ears' showing when you have tied your ballet shoes! 'Pigs' ears' are the two little ends of ribbon that show at the back of the ankle after you have tied up your ballet shoes – these should be tucked in under the ribbon – some dancers sew them in, before they go on stage. You see, if they show, they could get knocked and come undone and fall off.

Pirouettes   Turning while dancing.

Plié   A movement with the feet pointing sideways, with the knees bending over the toes (keeping the back straight).

Polka   A jaunty dance where the feet go 1-2-3 hop, 1-2-3 hop.

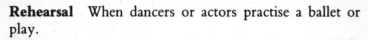

Prima ballerina
The principal star dancer.

Prop room   A room at the side or back of the stage where all the small objects (like mirrors, chairs, boxes, guitars, swords and so on) are stored until they are needed on stage by performers.

Rehearsal   When dancers or actors practise a ballet or play.

Répétiteur   The person who rehearses the soloists in the ballet.

Rosin tray   A tin tray on the floor containing sticky powder. Dancers rub their feet in it before they dance to stop them slipping. Ballet dancers also wet their heels

atter they have put on their tights, then stick the wet heel into the rosin tray before they put on their ballet shoes.

This is so that their ballet shoes will not slip off; they remain in place as if 'glued' to the heel.

Scenery   Pretend trees or houses, or ships or walls made out of canvas and wood and painted to look as if they were real.

Scenery dock   The large cave-like room at the back of the theatre where scenery is stored when it is not needed.

Skip   A large wicker basket, usually used to store costumes.

Solo   When only one dancer dances.

Spotlight   A powerful light that is shone from the back of the theatre and only shines on one performer at a time.

Stage   The raised platform in the theatre where the dancers or actors dance or sing or act.

Stage door-keeper   The man or woman who sits at the stage door (artists' entrance to the theatre) and takes messages for the dancers or actors, makes sure no one who should not be backstage gets by the door, and looks after all the keys for the dressing rooms. He or she also takes telephone messages (if he's in a good mood).

Star   The man or woman who has the most important part in a show and is the most famous.

Tabs Name for the huge curtains that fall in front of the stage.

Understudy The person who plays the part if a performer is ill and unable to go on stage.

Wardrobe mistress The person in charge of all the costumes in the theatre; seeing that the clothes are cleaned, repaired and kept looking as they did when they were first made.

Wings The side of the stage between the drapes (huge black curtains) where the artists stand and wait to go on stage.

A Selected List of Titles Available from Mammoth

While every effort is made to keep prices low, it is sometimes necessary to increase prices at short notice. Mammoth Paperbacks reserves the right to show new retail prices on covers which may differ from those previously advertised in the text or elsewhere.

The prices shown below were correct at the time of going to press.

☐	416 96490 7	**Dilly the Dinosaur**	Tony Bradman	£1.99
☐	749 70166 8	**The Witch's Big Toe**	Ralph Wright	£1.75
☐	416 95910 5	**The Grannie Season**	Joan Phipson	£1.75
☐	416 58270 2	**Listen to this Story**	Grace Hallworth	£1.75
☐	416 10382 0	**The Knights of Hawthorn Crescent**	Jenny Koralek	£1.50
☐	416 13882 5	**It's Abigail Again**	Moira Miller	£1.99
☐	749 70218 4	**Lucy Jane at the Ballet**	Susan Hampshire	£1.50
☐	416 06432 9	**Alf Gorilla**	Michael Grater	£1.75
☐	416 10362 6	**Owl and Billy**	Martin Waddell	£1.50
☐	416 13122 0	**Hetty Pegler, Half-Witch**	Margaret Greaves	£1.75
☐	749 70137 4	**Flat Stanley**	Jeff Brown	£1.99
☐	416 00572 1	**Princess Polly to the Rescue**	Mary Lister	£1.50
☐	416 00552 7	**Non Stop Nonsense**	Margaret Mahy	£1.75
☐	416 10322 7	**Claudius Bald Eagle**	Sam McBratney	£1.75
☐	416 03212 5	**I Don't Want To!**	Bel Mooney	£1.99

All these books are available at your bookshop or newsagent, or can be ordered direct from the publisher. Just tick the titles you want and fill in the form below.

Mammoth Paperbacks, Cash Sales Department, PO Box 11, Falmouth, Cornwall TR10 9EN.

Please send cheque or postal order, no currency, for purchase price quoted and allow the following for postage and packing:

UK   55p for the first book, 22p for the second book and 14p for each additional book ordered to a maximum charge of £1.75.

BFPO and Eire   55p for the first book, 22p for the second book and 14p for each of the next seven books, thereafter 8p per book.

Overseas Customers   £1.00 for the first book plus 25p per copy for each additional book.

NAME (Block letters) ....

ADDRESS ....

....